So Far From Forfar

Dan Makgow Smith

authorHOUSE®

AuthorHouse™
1663 Liberty Drive, Suite 200
Bloomington, IN 47403
www.authorhouse.com
Phone: 1-800-839-8640

First published by AuthorHouse 9/10/2010

ISBN: 978-1-4389-3031-2 (sc)
ISBN: 978-1-4389-3032-9 (hc)

Printed in the United States of America

This book is printed on acid-free paper.

*For those with Scottish blood flowing through their veins,
and have had the experience of finding the love of their
lives and losing it.*

Acknowledgments

This is my first novel, but not my last. This work took a lot out of me, as I at times struggled to find the next line to a sentence. There were other times though when I couldn't write fast enough to keep up with the thoughts that were flowing from my brain. The whole process though, was a true labor of love, as I found myself engulfed in the story as if I were writing about my own life.

I have a few people to thank, that made it possible to get this work to the printers and into the hands of readers like yourself.

My wife, Marti, who encouraged me and did abundant editing.

Bruce Wheeler, who gave me timely advise and took time to point me in the right direction.

Marty Teffeteller, who read my manuscript and made numerous corrections.

Melinda Davis, who edited my original draft— I hope it didn't scare you.

Sara Donald, thank you for taking time out of your schedule to read my manuscript and offer your valuable opinion.

Marla Osti, who did the final editing for me— I hope you finish your first book.

Grace Drown, who read my manuscript with a most enthusiastic approach.

R.J. McNall— If I could write as well as you paint, I'd be great!

. . . and especially for . . . you!

One

As the sun rose over the village of Forfar, the little Scottish community had already begun to stir. The town, being on the eastern side of Scotland, was one of the first villages to witness a new day in the making. Some of the villagers actually thought they themselves woke the sun! Shopkeepers were busy setting up their wares to sell or barter to either the locals or traveling patrons who happened to wander through this part of the country. Forfar was steeped rich in history, most of it very violent. Life was not easy, but the Scottish people, with their own brand of pride, were always able to rise above the challenges that confronted them.

Malcolm MacGow had grown up in this village as the son of a blacksmith having learned the trade from his father, Robert, who had learned it from his father. It was hard work but many rewards could be reaped from this type of work.

Malcolm was a muscular man and caused more than one of the local ladies to look his way on occasion. Many women desired to be the wife or at least the steady lady-friend of Malcolm so they could boast of the man they had. Another reward was the demand for his services because not too many people could handle this type of work or, for that matter, wanted to. Malcolm was born for this work. He could hardly wait for each day to begin as he looked upon his job as a calling from his ancestors to continue a tradition that spanned the history of Scotland itself. Malcolm had been taught a lot of history orally, as it was the Scottish way to pass along tales from the past regarding how their people came into being. He was familiar with the famous battle of North Inch in 1396, a rivalry involving the Clan Chattan and Clan MacPherson. Inter-clan battles were very common ways to settle disputes, but at other times were fought solely for the purpose of taking what belonged to someone else. What made this battle unique to Malcolm was that a man named Henry Wynd of Perthshire was hired to do battle on one side of the conflict for a certain amount of gold. Henry, known as Henry Gow or Henry the blacksmith, took to the fight so well that after killing one man, he sat down and declared his part of the bargain fulfilled.

The promise of even greater rewards motivated Henry to continue and so he earned much gold that day by killing several more opponents and winning the day for his side. Henry was adopted into the Clan Chattan and became the progenitor of the Gow branch. To this day Malcolm is proud of his beginnings and it shows in his work each day.

"Dad, do you still want me to deliver this order to the Duncans?" Ian was a good son and as hard a worker as his father.

"Yes, that would be a good idea since we will be closed tomorrow for the Sabbath. Just make sure Mr. Duncan signs for the order and is satisfied with it."

"Okay Dad, I'm on my way."

Ian was Malcolm's right-hand man as well as his son. He couldn't imagine not having him around to do all the running chores like delivery, supply pick-ups, and other odds and ends that freed Malcolm up for the hardcore smithing. Having a twenty-one year old around made this a perfect working team. Many people depended on Malcolm to keep them in the iron goods necessary for everyday living. Of course, the chief of the clan that Malcolm belonged to, Clan Lindsay, was very dependent on him, especially for the weapons he produced to outfit his clansmen for battle.

Malcolm had been in only a few clan battles in his time and had actually taken a life on several occasions. He kept his warrior skills honed by constant practice and by teaching his son, Ian, the art of warfare. Ian himself had been in only one battle so far in his life, but one never knew when the next confrontation would arise. This was the way life was in the 1600's. Therefore young men had to know how to do battle and more importantly, how to survive. Protecting the chief and doing his bidding was part of living on the chief's land—it was part of the agreement of being a partaker of the kindness of the chief. After all, it was his land.

Upon returning from his delivery, Ian was eager to find out what his next assignment would be. Ian and his father kept very busy with the forge, fulfilling the orders of the village. They depended on each other, particularly since there was no lady in the household to perform the womanly duties around the house. Malcolm's wife had gone out on her own years ago right after their son Ian was old enough to fend for himself and make it on his own. Malcolm learned to deal with this, but still longed for female company on occasion.

"Dad, are you still here?" Ian called out to Malcolm in the barn.

"I'm over here in the last stall tending to the Cobbs' horse. They've ridden this mare far too long before seeing to this loose shoe. I think with a little ointment, she'll be good as new in a few days time. She's a good horse and has many years left in her."

"I ran into an old friend of yours coming out of the tavern on my way back from the Duncans. Remember Alasdair Downie from the upper portion of the Strathmore Valley? He said he needs to see you soon with some important information."

"I wonder what he needs to see me about; I haven't seen or talked to him in over a year, if I remember correctly. Well, that's got me curious for sure. Last I heard of him, he was studying to obtain his license to practice law. He was always a very thorough man in business affairs and I suspect he will make a fine lawyer," Malcolm said. "Ian, it appears that we've fallen behind in our orders, but I'm sure we'll be able to meet our deadlines if we work as a team and put in a few more hours. I've got a lot of irons in the fire, if you'll excuse the expression. I'm leading a party of investors into the Highlands in a few days, and that will be time consuming all by itself, but they're paying me handsomely for the trip and I can't turn it down."

"Don't worry, Dad, I'll keep things running until you return and tend to the customer orders as fast as I can. I may be a little slow on the deliveries, but I'll catch up when you return."

"I'm sure you'll do your best. Just keep our regulars happy and we'll do what we can for the visitors."

Malcolm always worried about what his son thought and felt about his mother leaving so abruptly. She apparently was more interested in her newfound friends and their outlandish ways and parties than keeping house. He knew he had done his best in bringing Ian along through life and teaching him not only a trade, but how to deal with the obstacles that were either set in front of him or just managed to appear from nowhere. Ian had managed well and never complained too much. Malcolm, knowing his own disposition, could never have done as well. As busy as his work kept him, he still had time to consider his own loneliness when things got quiet—not that he felt sorry for himself . . . but he was human.

Forfar was situated in the center of the kingdom of the Picts. The Picts were the first settlers in the region, which eventually became known as Scotland. They made up one fourth of the peoples of Scotland before they all were united under one banner. Malcolm's father taught him about their own personal history and what part they played through the centuries to the forming of this great country. Malcolm was proud of his heritage even though there always seemed to be a clan battle taking place somewhere. His father, Robert, taught him about how blacksmiths had come along with the first people who settled Scotland because clans always had to have weapons to defend themselves. When they came to a strange land and not knowing what or who might confront the tribe made having a person who could make a weapon quite necessary.

The early Celtic people also brought the Druids— religious men and women who were leaders among the people and who gave the law that they all lived by. Malcolm made a point of teaching Ian just how close the smiths and the Druids were to each other. Some of the most skilled weapon makers were members of the priesthood. Druid smiths, it was said, produced magical swords, creating steel weapons far more superior then an iron blade. They would actually mix their own blood in the making of their swords to temper the steel.

"Ian, have I told you how our family got its name?"

"No, Dad, I don't believe you have. We've always been referred to as 'blacksmith,' 'smithy,' or the like."

"Well, son, our name originally was 'Mac a Ghobhainn'; it means 'son of the smith.' Ghobhainn means 'Smith' but sometimes is shortened to just Smith. In the Old Celtic, the name was Goban.The term 'smithcraft' was also used in referring to us."

"We really were— are— important to the clan, aren't we, Dad?"

"Yes, son, we still are, but there's more to us, I mean our immediatefamily, that I haven't shared with you."

"Like what, Dad?"

"In due time, Ian, in due time."

Malcolm was hesitant to tell him what was on his mind concerning his own father Robert and the role he had played in the family before he died. However, Malcolm knew that his son had a right to know the secret he held. After all, his son was of his blood and that of his grandfather as well. How would he react though? What would he do with this new information? He knew he had to tell him though and very soon.

Not only did Malcolm do a lot of horseshoing and sword making, but he also gave horseback riding lessons. He had a good reputation as a horseman, which made him very popular as an instructor also. He had many clients who paid him to learn the art of riding such a beast. He enjoyed teaching them and helping them overcome their fear of a big animal. This was also a way of supplementing his income since times were tough.

As Malcolm went about his day at the stables, he noticed someone, a woman he had never seen before, sitting on a rail by the barn. Malcolm made a point of working his way over to where she sat just to make conversation with her. The more he watched her, the more she lit up the area with her beauty. Malcolm was mesmerized and wanted to get to know her.

"Hi, I'm Malcolm MacGow. Are you interested in learning about the horses?"

"Hello, I'm Kate MacPherson. I'm not very good at this kind of thing, and I just want to sit here and watch. It makes me nervous when other people watch me. I'm very private."

"There's nothing to worry about. No one is watching you; they're here to learn themselves. I'll tell you what; next time you come by, I'll give you a free lesson. Sound okay?"

"Let me think about it first. I'll let you know."

"Okay, I hope to see you again."

Malcolm went about his business, but just could not get her out of his mind. He could not wait until he saw her again. He even made a promise to himself that he would not let his emotions run away with him. She was just a nice girl that he had run into, and he would help her just like any other student.

The days ahead kept him busy with his work in the blacksmith shop and the horseback riding lessons, but still he had one person on his mind. Every day he would strain his eyes and hope to catch her coming by, even in the distance, just so he could get a glimpse of her. Why was she so alluring to him? What was it about her that so attracted him to her?

Two

Malcolm was getting his gear prepared for his trip to the northern part of the Highlands to lead a group of investors who wanted to build roads to make the area more accessible. Trying to get other clans to cooperate with this plan was not going to be an easy task. Many people in the village wanted to keep things as they were and saw no reason for change, while others wanted better access to southern areas to deliver their cattle to market. Malcolm saw only the opportunity to open up the region and increase the business opportunities in Forfar.

He was again going to do his best with these investors and get paid handsomely for it. Although he was generally tied to his shop, he had from time to time ventured out on his own to hunt or explore the northern area he was going to again.

"Ian, this was a good breakfast you've prepared this morning, better than usual. What's the occasion?"

"I figure you're not going to eat as well the next several days, so I did a little bit extra this morning. Besides, it gives me a chance to practice my culinary talents."

"I don't know where you picked up your cooking abilities, but I do know that it wasn't from me!"

On his way to meet up with the investors, Malcolm decided to make a side trip to see Alasdair Downie, his longtime friend who wanted to see him. By horseback, the Killiemuir area was not that far out of the way, and besides, he wasn't to meet with his party for several hours from now. Making his way through the forested area of Forfar actually cut his travel time considerably, rather than taking the more traveled road. He had missed this area he was traversing now; it had been awhile since he had moved through this forest while doing some hunting. It was good to be back here again. As he cleared the wooded area, he could see crofts and other structures of business just some twenty miles from Forfar and knew he had arrived. The town he remembered still looked the same, not quite as big as his own, but still of good size. As he rode down the street, he looked for familiar faces he could inquire as to where Alasdair's home might be. He stopped and talked to a gentleman who was busy with a load of lumber. "Could you direct me to Alasdair Downie's place?"

"Aye, just down a little ways, then turn to your right at the big oak and he's a stone's throw down on the left."

"Thank you, kind sir."

Meandering down the road, Malcolm found the oak tree and made his turn as directed. There, just down the street, he saw the shingle of 'Alasdair Downie, Esq.'

"I guess he did pass the bar; well good for him," exclaimed Malcolm. Tying his horse to the post, he made his way to the front door and gently pushed it open.

"Good day, Sir, could I . . . Malcolm! Malcolm MacGow, how good it is to see you again, my friend. " He scooted his chair back and stood to shake Malcolm's hand.

"Aye, it's good to see you once again too. It's been too long. What's it been, a year or more?"

"At least that long. Here, let me offer you a drink— Scotch?"

"Ha, Ha! What else would you offer a Scotsman,?"

"Here you are, old friend, Uisge Breathe, the 'water of life."

"This is just what I needed to wash down the dust of the last few miles."

"Did Ian give you the message to see me?"

"That he did. He said you had important information for me. Is it really that urgent?"

"I think it is, Malcolm. Do you remember a man named Theodore Higginbottom?His history dates back to the 1660's during the witch trials. He was the chief prosecutor of the trials which put so many people, witch or not, to death."

"I believe Dad did mention someone like that when he passed on some very private family information to me. The trials took place in my hometown of

Forfar. What does this have to do with me now?"

"Just this: in studying for my exams for this profession, I came across his name in some old documents related to the witch trials. He wasn't too particular about who he accused of being a witch or a sympathizer. One of those people was . . . your father! Actually, it was Higginbottom's son who made the accusation."

"My father? He was no witch. My father was not a witch.""I'm sure he wasn't, but Theodore's son Joel made your father very angry. Words were exchanged and Joel challenged your father to a duel. Your father beat Joel in that duel, killing him on the spot. Never fight with a blacksmith, I've always said."

"Why didn't Mr. Higginbottom pursue the charges against my father?"

"It seems that the witch trials were winding down and public interest was waning. They were tired of the killing and were suspicious of the manner in which some of the victims were charged. Luckily for your father, I don't believe Mr. Higginbottom had the support to continue."

"I know I can trust you, Alasdair, and what I'm about to tell you must remain in strict confidence. Like I said, my father was not a witch, but he was connected to a sect of the Druids. He had been taught the Druid way from very early on just like his father had. From what I can understand, he never did complete his training but possessed a lot of knowledge of the art and earned the protection of the Druids all of his life. It was during the time of the killing of Higginbottom's son that the Druids came to the rescue of my father from any more personal attacks on his character. Certain Druid 'agents' were sent out to talk with Theodore Higginbottom to persuade him to cease any action against my father. They also told Mr. Higginbottom that he would feel safer outside of Scotland— in other words, leave the country."

"I think I know where Theodore Higginbottom went— to the British colony, America! This brings me, Malcolm, to the rest of the story that I'm telling you. Seeing that Mr. Higginbottom and myself are both in the profession of the law, I thought you should know that I've had a letter reach my office recently and the contents spell out the same pattern of witch hunting that took place thirty years ago in Forfar, perpetrated by this same Mr. Higginbottom. It is now resurfacing in the colony there known as Massachusetts."

"My brother Daniel is in that colony! He set sail two years ago in 1691, and I've yet to hear back from him. This is a very disturbing turn of events."

Three

America was far different from Daniel's Scotland. There was the absence of old buildings that dominated the landscape as they did in Forfar and the bigger towns back home. Not as many people populated the area. There were vast open expanses of wilderness yet to be explored, plenty of room to roam. He was enjoying Salem though, especially in summer. It was a lot hotter in Massachusetts than anywhere in his native land, but it was a pleasant change of climate for Daniel. Oh, but the winters here were most terrible, even harsher than back home. But Daniel adapted and went on with his business. What was his business though? He knew he could always blacksmith. There's always need of a smithy, but he could have stayed home and done that. No, he wanted something more rewarding, something he could make his fortune at, and he found just that: exploring and trapping in this vast wilderness. Heading west, the horizon never seemed to end. No matter how far he traveled west, there was always more land beyond. He had already amassed a small fortune in the brief time since he had arrived, and there seemed to be no end to what he could accomplish. Daniel had arrived back in the Boston area with a full load of pelts and Indian items he had traded for and felt very happy with his latest venture.

"Do you have enough deer hides to do me for the next two months?" the store owner Mr. Barclay called to Daniel as he saw him coming up the well traveled dirt road.

"I've got enough to do you for the next six months, you old goat! You know

I always give you first crack at my spoils."

"That's good to hear, as long as the price is right."

"If you buy the whole lot, I'll give you the best deal this side of the Hudson."

"Well, let me take a look at 'em first. I ain't got all day."

Daniel was well connected to the right buyers and had been trading with them for the past two years, gaining the reputation of being able to deliver the goods they needed for their customers. Daniel had been able to buy a fine cottage in Salem and was regarded by other local businessmen as a fine example of Scottish thriftiness. He loved the excitement of the hunt and the freedom of the great outdoors. He had found a way to be hospitable to the native Indian groups, which was necessary in order to conduct his business on their land. He hadn't even thought about returning to Scotland in light of his success here, but he often thought about his brother Malcolm.

There were troubles in Salem though, but they didn't concern him. He was not too religious, and the problems seemed to be church- related anyway. He kept to himself most of the time and worked on his piece of land, chopping wood and storing up for the next winter. The extra furs he didn't sell would keep him warm in the terrible cold weather that would fall upon them all too soon.

The only thing that bothered Daniel was that he should have come to the colonies sooner. At least he was here now and would make the best of it. The Scots were ingenious and well able to adapt to their surroundings. They were fierce fighters, which came in handy when dealing with people who were warlike themselves. Daniel kept an even temperament though and if given a choice always took peace over conflict.

Daniel's travels, in his fur trapping, had taken him to new and strange locations many miles from civilization. He had always been adventurous back in Scotland and would roam the hills and glens just to see what was there. He always loved hunting and relished the thought of being known as a great hunter. The family never wanted for meat on the table as long as he was around. With a bit of pride, he wondered what his brother back home was doing for meat. He knew Malcolm didn't have as much time to hunt as he did and thought he must be eating lots of oatmeal. He snickered at the thought but knew his brother was able to take care of the home front as well.

As the night came on, Daniel already had his fire burning, preparing a stew that others would kill for just to get a taste. Being a great cook gave him an advantage in staving off the hunger pains. Vegetables were really the only thing he had to buy since he didn't have the time to tend a garden these days, and they could be kept fresh in underground storage areas.People were always willing to barter for the furs and meat he traded, so they all benefitted from each other.

After a hearty supper, Daniel decided to head for the local inn, where an occasional bottle of spirits could be purchased to take the chill off and the men would sit around and swap stories of their daily activities. Many things could be learned from these sessions and many a tale would be embellished, according to how much the storyteller had to drink. There were as many conversations going on at the inn as there were tables. Daniel was known as the hunter-trapper in the area and was always sought after to deliver a tale from the frontier, as many of the men did not venture too far from Salem proper. Daniel would have their attention and didn't have to stretch the truth much as his tales were exciting enough as they happened. The news Daniel liked hearing the most was from newcomers who had arrived from the old country. He wanted to know what wars were taking place, what the Crown had decreed regarding the colonies that might affect him, and who of importance had died.

"Laddie, what news have ya from county Cork, if anything?" said one of the patrons with his fist full of whiskey.

The newcomer was taken by surprise that anyone would speak to him, seeing that he knew no one here.

"Well, lads, I am from Ireland but not from county Cork. I'm from Cavan and I can tell you that the hills are still green and the wenches fine, but the lack of jobs and proper food is too much for many of us. You men did well to come here, I'm sure."

Daniel took it all in as he sipped his drink and remained attentive to the conversation. It wasn't uncommon for men to leave Scotland, Ireland, or England to come to the new world. Some came for better opportunities to help support their families and some like himself came for the adventure and making some money.

"Are there more yet to come from abroad to this land?" said another patron.

"Aye, there be more for sure. I was lucky enough to get the farewhen I did. Some even resorted to a bit of violence to sail."

"And what of Scotland, my good man? What hear ye from there?"

"They have the same problem as we Irish and many there be that will make the trip when they can. I hate to fix blame, but the English make it terribly difficult on people. I mean they treat those of us not from England not so well, as second class citizens at best."

"They for sure are a power unto themselves and control the seas. They have always wanted to control the island that Scotland is a part of. I hate not the

Englishman, but his government is something else altogether. Why can't we have the peace we deserve and need?" spoke another man sitting at one of the tables.

As they spoke and compared opinions, others were coming and going as the night moved on. Many spoke of simply having a piece of land and raising a family without interference from anyone. They wanted to worship their God and enjoy life with friends. They looked toward the future and sought peace with their neighbors and wanted to be left alone by the government. They just wanted freedom.

"Daniel, I admire the fact that you have the time to get away out in the wilderness and enjoy the countryside," spoke an old-timer slowly taking a drink from his cup. "If I had my legs again, I'd join you on some of those long treks you take."

"Well, I'd love to have you along, but I tell you what, next timeout, I'll bring you back a set of deer antlers like you never seen before. How about that?"

"I'd like that very much, Daniel. I'd like that very much."

The evening was getting late as Daniel decided to call it a night and get home to his cottage. He needed time to let all the talk of this night sink in so he could make educated decisions about what he had heard. As he finished his drink and was getting up to leave, the door of the inn burst open with force as three men of official-looking nature stood looking around the room.

"We would speak with one Daniel MacGow. Is he here?"

Patrons, stunned at the obtrusive nature of these gentlemen, looked at each other and finally at Daniel, saying nothing.

"Well, is he among you or not?"

"I am he; I am Daniel MacGow. What is this about, if I may ask?"

"The chief prosecutor Theodore Higginbottom requests your company at this time; please come with us."

"I'm afraid I haven't the time to visit this night. Tell Mr. Higginbottom it will have to be on another date."

"And I'm afraid you have no choice. We have an arrest warrant for you. Will you come peacefully or . . . ?"

"An arrest warrant on what charge?"

"Ignoring the Sabbath . . . and cavorting with familiar spirits onyour 'trips' to the woods. Seems this sort of thing runs in your family."

Four

"He could cause my brother untold harm if he identifies him," Malcolm said to Alasdair. "I need to get a letter off to him as soon as possible. Can you help me with that?"

"I'd be most happy to do that," Alasdair said, eagerly complying with Malcolm's request. "I'll need to be discreet though so as not to alert the wrong people and possibly make matters worse."

"I would greatly appreciate that, Alasdair. I don't know if he is actually in danger, but I do feel an urgency to communicate with him."

"Look, there's nothing more you can do at this time, so why don't you take your mind off of this for now and get on with your trek into the mountains?"

"You're right, of course; I'll do just that. When I'm done, I'll be going back to Forfar if you need me."

"Very good. Try not to let this bother you. You, too, have a life. Besides, it's going to be some time before we know anything."

Malcolm led the investors to the area they desired so they could conduct their business. They spent almost a week on this journey, and Malcolm could sense they were exuberant about what they once saw there. Most of them were not accustomed to outdoor activities such as this, but they did their best and set their minds to the task at hand. Some of them couldn't wait to get back to civilization to take a hot bath and get into their usual change of clean clothes. They had carried most of the food stores they needed so Malcolm only had to kill minimally for meat along the way. With the wages they were paying

Malcolm, he would be able to buy a new stallion that he would present to his son, Ian, on his next birthday. He felt that Ian deserved to be repaid for all he had done to help Malcolm and make him the successful blacksmith that he was. He knew Ian would greatly appreciate this and couldn't wait to see the look on his face at that time.

Upon their arrival back in Killiemuir, Malcolm said his good-byes to the investors and received his pay for the trip.

"Good day, gentlemen. I hope your time wasn't wasted and that your venture is a successful one."

"And we thank you, kind sir. If your services are ever needed again, we'll look you up."

Malcolm was eager to return home and tell Ian of the possible trouble that Daniel could be facing in America. He rode like a man possessed as he spared no delicate flower that his horse might trample in the paths he took. He thought it funny that life could deal him a blow that he never saw coming when he thought he had everything under control and was the master of his life's direction. He was finding out that sometimes circumstances can take you in directions you might not have foreseen. Malcolm thought about growing up with his brother, the typical things that boys do and how they would get in trouble and have to face their father when they got caught. He remembered once when Daniel sneaked into old man MacNab's field and tried to ride his prize stallion, accidentally letting him get away and run to the next county. Not only did Daniel have to apologize to Mr. MacNab, but his father made him do chores at MacNab's ranch for a month to make amends.

Even though Malcolm was five years older than Daniel, he too had his own share of mischief to contend with. He was supposed to be setting an example for his younger brother but sometimes was more of a bad example for him. Malcolm could daydream forever about the tiffs and predicaments they both had gotten themselves into at times, but that was long ago and they were both now grown and responsible men, brothers who looked out for each other no matter what. It was at this time though that Malcolm felt helpless to assist his brother in a time of possible need.

Upon arriving back in Forfar, Malcolm made his way to his barn at the blacksmith shop. Before Malcolm could see his son Ian, he heard him, pounding away on the anvil with a loud reverberating clang that sounded like chimes of an enormous clock announcing the time of day.

"Dad," Ian cried out to his father, "you made it back!"

"Of course I made it back! You see me, don't you?"

Dismounting from his tired horse, father and son embraced with a strong bear hug as only two blacksmiths could muster.

"No problems while I was away I take it."

"No sir, none at all, but..."

"But? But what?"

"There has been this lady who has come by several times and just watches the horses and the riders as they practice their jumps and exercises."

"Did you talk to her to see what she wanted? What did she look like?"

"Very pretty and very eye catching; somewhere around forty years old or so I guess."

Malcolm knew exactly who he was describing, but didn't let on. He knew it was Kate MacPherson, probably ready to take the horse-back riding lessons she had talked about. It was also Malcolm's opportunity to see the woman that he couldn't forget about. She had made such an impression on him right after their first meeting that he was as eager to see her again and anticipating it more than anything he could think of. He was smitten for sure, even as fast as a rattler could strike.

"Let's go get some supper; I'm hungry enough to eat a horse. I hope our menagerie didn't hear that," Malcolm laughed out loud to Ian.

"I'll whip us up something good and hearty. Besides, who would want to eat horse if they didn't have to?"

After Malcolm put his horse away and fed him, he set his sights on a good relaxing meal and some good conversation with his son. He knew it was time to fill him in on some of the family secrets concerning his own father, Ian's grandfather.

As always, Ian had made a small feast fit for a king, at least it tasted that way to Malcolm after the long ride home. After taking seconds on everything he could and washing it down with some home-made wine, he was prepared to talk to Ian but didn't know where to start. Why not at the beginning, he thought.

"Ian, pull up a chair and make yourself comfortable; it's time we talked."

Five

"I don't understand! Why am I in jail?" Daniel screamed.

"Somebody answer me! Is anybody out there?" Daniel strained his eyes to look first to the right and then to the left through the small window bars of his cell. The corridor of jail cells all looked the same with heavy wooden doors and strong bolts and hinges to keep their prisoners or in jail from escaping. Having been whisked away from his place of freedom to this desolate jail cell had not sat well with Daniel. Apparently, the clergy wielded much power in this community and had the power to accuse and arrest people they deemed to be problems.

"I've nothing to do with these people. Why am I mixed up with their problems? Maybe they have the wrong man. Someone made a mistake on the warrant. What's this all about?" Daniel talked out loud to himself.

"Brother, have you been falsely accused as well? I have been here two days now and have not talked to anyone. They bring me food and drink, not very tasty, but enough to keep me alive," said someone in a cell across and down from Daniel. "These men are evil and know not the God of the Bible. I feel not the spirit within them for they are cruel, vulgar men who know only pain and death."

"Why do they do what they do?" Daniel asked.

"They are led by wild ugly power and relish controlling others who they say are possessed by the devil. The love of God is not in them. They cause good men to say things that are not true and persuade others to follow their madness out of ignorance or fear."

"I know God, but this place is insane. I was not raised this way, but with love toward my fellow man. What do they plan on doing with us?"

"My brother, they have put to death many already, and many more await their sentences even as we speak. Some have been burned at the stake, others drowned, and many tortured to death for not being able to disprove the claims of witchcraft. It's a mass hysteria affecting the whole village. They seem eager to convict people, like they're some sort of religious zealots."

"I've got to get out of here. I'm not dying for any religious cause or for any other reason. If I can get past these walls, I'll head to the wilderness and hide among the Indians friends I've made there."

"And what of us, my brother. What will the innocent women who are still to die going to do? Will you leave them to face certain death by these madmen?"

Daniel stopped his ranting for a minute to consider what the fellow prisoner had said. He's right, he thought to himself. I just can't run and let more people die at the hands of those butchers. I've got to come up with a plan to try and end all this. What can I do all alone? If I can get away, maybe I can have time to think of a way, devise a plan, and return to help them. I wish I were back in Scotland with my brother. Why did my world turn upside down all of a sudden? Maybe I should have stayed a blacksmith.

"Tomorrow I start the trial of Daniel MacGow. It's such a small world we live in. Did the MacGows think I would be thwarted forever? I've a long memory and have not forgotten how my son was murdered by that Malcolm back in Scotland. I'll make Malcolm rue the day he crossed my path and caused me to have to leave my homeland of Britain or my name's not Theodore Higginbottom. Isn't that right, Marcus?"

"Yes, sir, you are correct, sir," said Marcus, Higginbottom's assistant. "It is my pleasure to serve and assist you in this most glorious endeavor. Glory to God."

As Theodore Higginbottom's staff collected their "facts" and made ready the new accusations to be revealed to the villagers, Daniel too was making his plan of escape in order to assure his continued existence on God's green earth. Having been a blacksmith, he knew how metal hinges and parts were constructed and how to take advantage of their weaknesses. From his own beltbuckle, he was able to construct a tool to force the hinge pin out of its holding position and compromise the integrity of the door's strength. It wasn't going to be easy, but he thought he could figure out a way to pry the door away from the frame. Daniel was resourceful, desperate and at this point a fighter, as taught by his father and brother. No pudgy clergyman was going to have his way with him and, if he could help it, no one else either. He had come to this continent to make his way in life and pursue his dreams and that's just what he was going to do.

As he was planning his way out of this prison, he heard the main door to the compound open with a loud creak and the noise of dangling keys as two men came in and made their way to a cell just past his. Opening the door they called out, "Mr. Jacobs, get up. You've a trial to attend, you son of perdition." Seeing that Jacobs was not eager to attend such a meeting, they called out to several men who awaited their command. "Guards! Guards! Extract this one and take him to the meeting hall."

As the guards pulled Mr. Jacobs from his cell and began dragging him out, Daniel looked out of his cell door window and clinched his fist tightly around the bars as his face distorted with rage, unable to help the feeble old man from his tormentors. He watched as they left the room and the door slammed shut behind them with the resonating echo of the fading voice of their next victim. Daniel walked back to the wall in his cell and began pacing to relieve the tension that had built up in him over the incident that had just taken place. He kicked the cot and slammed his drinking cup against the wall in frustration. Still unable to completely understand the whole scenario, Daniel racked his brain to try and make as much sense of these past twenty-four hours as he could. He contemplated his plan of attack when he could free himself from his confinement. He knew he couldn't take the chance of going to a trial and pleading ignorance in light of what the other prisoner had told him. That would be suicide on his part. He had to get away from this area to have time to formulate a plan. His mind went back to the old man being led away to probably what would turn out to be his execution. If only he was out and able to wield his sword again. He would at least go down fighting and take as many of them with him as he could. Maybe he could spur an uprising of sorts and turn the tide of opposition against this group of illegitimate clergy. If he had known the situation a little better at the time of his arrest, he would have put up a fight and would have not have been taken at all. He had trusted the system and had merely been cooperating with the established authority. He now realized the folly of that decision.

"Brother, you must pray with me concerning this dire matter," said the man in the other cell. "We must call upon the Lord to fight for us and deliver us from evil men."

"Yes, that we must do, but I'm also putting feet to my prayers and trying to get us out of here. If I can get away, it's possible I can figure out how to help us all. I need time to work this hinge, so pardon me if I get too involved with this work."

Daniel got busy on his escape. He used his belt buckle in a way that it was not intended to operate, but that was the advantage of being one who worked with metal. He often had to devise quick fixes to help a customer who had an implement that was broken and needed mending. As Daniel worked on loosening the door, he talked to the other prisoner.

"How long was Mr. Jacobs in here?"

"George Jacobs had been in here since May. May 10th to be exact. What a horrible curse that has come upon us," said the fellow prisoner. "I suspect that it's no curse at all but simple mad men exercising power over the flock and instilling fear as a weapon against you."

"Surely no one is that cruel. I pray God they're not."

"I can tell you this: we went through a similar experience in Scotland some thirty years back. Almost identical . . . almost . . . identical," Daniel thought aloud. The more he thought about it, there was something very familiar about this. He thought to himself concerning this matter and felt like he had been through it before. A story had been related to him many years ago and had not caused him to think anything of it, but now something was whispering to him in his own mind. He and Malcolm both had been told the story by their father years previous, regarding their connection with the Druid priests. Was this connected in any way? He didn't see how, but still . . . that feeling, a feeling of association with the past. How did it connect? What part did he have in this scheme? Daniel continued working on the hinges and was making progress with the old doors.

"There! I finally got the bolt loose enough to pull out." As he gripped the bolt with all of his strength, he tugged it completely out and dropped it on the floor at his feet. Breathing hard now and wiping the perspiration from his face, he started on the middle hinge and went through the same process. It was tedious work that taxed the forearms of his strong frame, but he didn't know how much time he had before they might come for him. The second hinge was somewhat easier because of the placement, and out it came as well. Sweat dripped annoyingly as he worked on the bottom hinge. He had to keep wiping his forehead, which also made his hands slippery.

The bottom bolt was the toughest because it held more of the weight, and that just compounded Daniel's work effort. Fortunately, he was a strong man and was able to hold the weight of the door as he pried the last bolt from the door and allowed it to lean against the frame. Daniel knew that time was of the essence and made his way to the outside door to test it.

"Locked, as I guessed. I'll have to wait until someone opens it from the outside and make my move at that time." Rushing back to the prisoner he had been talking to, he called to him through the cell bars. "Hello, are you awake?"

"I'm awake, just praying that you don't get caught on this bold move of yours."

"I may have to fight my way out of here but hopefully something else will happen to make it easier."

"Get word to my wife that I'm ok for now, can you do that?"

"Where do you live or where may I find her?"

"She's staying with our friends because it's safer that way. They are right near the edge of town by the river in a bigger cottage due to their large family. Please get to her for me. Tell her I'll be alright, God willing."

"I'll do my best; keep the faith." Daniel waited behind where the door would open so that when the constable returned, he would be able to make his move. He noticed several other prisoners looking out of their cell door windows at him where he took up position. They were eager to see what would happen when the time came. They kept quiet and watched along with Daniel as the time slowly crept by. Feeling fatigued, Daniel sat down in his spot and continued to wait. Prisoners took turns resting and then looking out again to see what Daniel was doing to pass the time. Daniel alternately bowed his head, scribbled in the dirt floor with a stick, huffed and puffed and threw his head back against the wall in frustration. He knew it was going to be dangerous work very soon, and the waiting was just making him anxious. Daniel was just about to nod off to sleep when he was suddenly startled back to reality by the sound of keys in the door. He jumped to his feet and prepared to do whatever necessary to secure his freedom. As the heavy door began to swing open, he saw a booted leg enter just past the door. He stayed hidden as well as he could and watched the men walk down the dirt floor toward the cells at the far end. It was at this point that he rounded the door and headed toward the exit to freedom, preparing for whatever he had to face on the other side. "You there, stop! In the name of the High Constable, I command you to halt," said one of the men in the group who had just entered.

Six

"Some things have come to light, Ian, that I need to discuss with you. Oh, by the way, that was a delicious meal, son," said Malcolm.

"Thanks, Dad. I enjoy the opportunity to practice on you," Ian laughed to his dad.

"Make sure there's plenty of wine just in case," Malcolm said, returning the laugh. "But right now I have to bring you up to date on family business— business that you have the right to know as you embrace your heritage.

"Years ago, your grandfather, Robert, practiced his religion in the Druid fashion. He had been taught this way since he was a boy, and this practice has been in our family for many generations. It basically stopped with me," Malcolm said. "Father thought it time to end as times were changing and Christianity was far more prevalent in Scotland. My father had never actually completed the training even though he was very close to his Druid brothers. They fully accepted him in every other way."

"Dad, how much did he reveal to you of this practice?"

"Hardly anything really. He taught me many things concerning it, but not enough to practice the art itself."

"I have heard of the Druids and their ways from friends and others and always felt that they did good work even though it was not Christian. Is this true?"

"Oh yes, very true indeed. Although the Druids basically disappeared over some fifteen hundred years ago, certain sects of them continued to practice their religion but only in small circles of influence. The Druids were good people and instructed the others about the growing season so they would know when to plant and harvest. This practice is still going on today all over Britain."

"I do feel proud in knowing my own history is steeped in this lore. It seems that distortions concerning them are what people have come to fear," Ian said, sounding like a young man who was growing wise with knowledge.

"Your grandfather had a duel with a man who falsely accused him of being connected with witchcraft. This was what Alasdair Downie needed to tell me. It concerns the man responsible for the witch trials here in Forfar thirty years ago. He's now in America where Daniel is."

"So if he makes the connection with Daniel and my grandfather, he could cause trouble," Ian said.

"Alasdair is sending a letter off to the Colonies in hopes of alerting Daniel. Unfortunately, that's the best we can do now."

"You know, Dad, there have been several witches executed even after the trials in the '60's, but nothing like that three year span back then."

"You are right. They have become sporadic but have not completely disappeared."

At this time, someone began to knock on Malcolm's front door. "I'll get it," said Ian. Walking to the front door, Ian opened it and saw Jabel Bruce, the local clergyman.

"Reverend! What brings you out at this late hour?"

"Is Malcolm at home? I need to talk to him."

"Yes, he's right here. Come in, please."

"Is anything the matter, Reverend Bruce?"

"Earlier tonight I received a visitor at my church who was very mysterious but had something to say that I don't fully understand. He said you are in danger and are being watched."

"Watched? By whom?" Malcolm asked.

"By people who hold a grudge. By people who are evil by nature and never forget a wrongdoing. By people who have . . . killed your friend, Alasdair Downie."

"Alasdair's dead?" asked Malcolm.

"It seems that he had uncovered truths that were not meant to berevealed. He was killed this afternoon according to my visitor, not too long after you visited him."

"What am I not understanding here, Reverend?"

"I was the pastor to your father as well as you and your son. I knew the connection your father had with the Druids. I didn't judge him and never scolded him for what had been handed down to him through the ages concerning religious choices. I kept his secrets and became a good friend to your father and have always watched over your family, probably a little more than I have the other parishioners. Malcolm, it was a member of that same Druid sect that I talked to tonight. I'm sure the killers are not through yet. I don't know their plans, but I do believe that they want certain facts to remain hidden and not brought to light."

The Druid experience was becoming all too real to Ian, especially in light of what had been just said. He knew he was now part of this whole thing, whether he wanted to be or not. He also knew his life was never going to be the same and that this might be more excitement than he ever wanted. Nevertheless, he was propelled into it and was going to have to deal with it. He was not one to avoid his responsibilities and was ready to take his place.

"Ian, I'm sorry you had to be indoctrinated this way so soon, but now you know more than I intended to tell you. I'm still learning myself. Apparently there's more to this than I was even aware of."

"My friends, I would take this seriously and be on your guard. These people are ruthless and desperate to go to this extreme to shut someone up," Reverend Bruce said. "For all I know, they could be someone within my own congregation, in our own church, Heaven forbid."

"I just feel that my brother Daniel is somehow going to be mixed up in this, even way across the ocean. If only I could see him and talk to him. Reverend, what did the Druid look like? Could you identify him again?"

"Malcolm, I'm sorry, but no, I couldn't. He wore a hood and was basically covered from head to toe in a cape which shielded his face. He had an air of godliness about him though, I must admit. Kind of like talking to an angel. He spoke very clearly and commanded the room where we stood, and I knew he was who he said he was."

"Reverend, will you be all right from here on out?" Malcolm asked with concern.

"Oh, don't worry about me. I travel with God. Let men do what they wish, I'm in His hands. I'll be here for you and Ian in case you need anything. Feel free to come to me if you have any needs whatsoever. I'm sorry about Alasdair, may God rest his soul."

"I'll miss him very much. I should have not let so much time go between visits with him, Reverend."

"Well, good night and take care, Malcolm, Ian."

As Reverend Bruce left and walked on down the road, Malcolm thought about the things that had been told to him this night. Reverend Bruce disappeared around the bend in the road as the night stood silent once more. The moon and clouds made an eerie pattern in the night sky and gave the preceding conversation a somber meaning.

"Dad, what do we do now? Should we contact the local authorities tomorrow? Do we need protection?"

"I don't think they could really help us with this. I think the least said would be the wisest thing to do. Let's get some sleep. We'll look at it with new eyes on the morrow."

As Ian and Malcolm made ready for bed, Malcolm knew he wouldn't sleep long with so much on his mind. He wanted to keep Ian calm and wanted him to feel protected. Malcolm was beginning to realize what his own father had been up against now that these new events had come to light. He also knew that the forces which he had to contend with were well organized and had been performing their evil for a long time. When morning came, Ian was up first, after sleeping better than his father did. In spite of all that had happened yesterday, they still had a business to run. Customers depended on them, and they had to make a living. Malcolm was the only blacksmith in the area and kept a steady flow of jobs that only he and Ian could service. Malcolm and Ian did well and worked a full day, usually from sunup to nightfall. If they had to work late to finish a job, they would work by lantern.

"Ian, I'm going to skip breakfast and get out to the forge so I can get us caught up on the orders. You can join me when you get ready."

"I'm so hungry, I could eat for the both of us," Ian said. Ian, being a young man, would do just that, Malcolm thought.

As Malcolm got dressed and made his way to the barn to fire up the forge, he thought about his old friend, Alasdair. He had a lot on his mind and heart. However, he knew that he had to stop thinking of the current problems, and the best way to do that was to throw himself into his work so his mind would be occupied elsewhere. Ian had done a great job for him while he was gone, but it took two hardworking men to keep up with everything that had to be done in this work. By the time Malcolm got everything ready to begin, Ian was coming in to do his part of the work.

"Dad, I think we can get caught up and even be ahead in just a few days."

"Judging by what I can see, I think you may be right."

After working until around noon, Malcolm decided to take a break and get some food, as his hunger was starting to catch up with him. Gulping down a flask of water, he washed up and headed toward the cottage to grab some jerky and a little bread. As he was walking up the path toward home, he saw the lady who had introduced herself as Kate MacPherson coming toward him. His step began to move a little swifter and his heart beat faster as his whole attitude began to change, and suddenly, he was no longer hungry.

"Kate! It's good to see you again."

"Hello, Malcolm! It's good to see you again too. I thought I might try the riding lessons if you have the time." Malcolm would make time for her. This reunion had just made his day. Something about her made Malcolm perk up and take notice. His mind was racing so fast that he was having trouble organizing his thoughts to even talk to her.

"I'd be glad to teach you. Are you sure you won't be too shy to have others watch you? They're really not watching you so much as they are just trying to learn themselves, so no need to be self-conscious."

"I'll just follow your lead then and let you guide me. I've never done anything like this before."

"Okay then. Let me get some of the paperwork out of the way and make you a schedule so we can keep track of our progress. By the way, there will be no charge for you. It's on me, okay?"

"Thank you very much. I really appreciate this. Am I dressed alright for the training?"

"You're just fine. As long as you're comfortable and can freely move, that should be fine." Malcolm was feeling somewhat nervous. He had never reacted this way with other clients. He was gradually moving into an area that he wasn't looking to go, by some unseen force pushing him toward . . . toward what? He had not been looking for anyone like this and had not even thought about any kind of relationship with anyone, but she most definitely had his attention.

As time went on, Kate was making progress with her riding skills and felt that she was really on her way to achieving her goals. After she had made significant gains in her riding, she started to feel an attraction toward Malcolm, but didn't tell him so right away. After a lesson one day, Malcolm and Kate began to have a casual conversation about their personal lives.

"Malcolm, I haven't told you before, but I'm engaged to a gentleman whom I have known for some time now. It has been a long engagement, and I'm not so sure about things. Things just aren't the way I think they should be between us. There's something missing that he just doesn't provide."

"But still you're with him. What keeps you there?"

"Oh, there are other issues like security and the fact that I've been with him for so long. I think if I left him, he'd probably go crazy." "What about you though? What about your feelings and the things you're missing out on in life? Doesn't that count for anything?" Malcolm replied.

"I am tired of not putting myself first when I ought to. There are times when I need to look out for myself for a change."

"Well, there are things I'm missing too in life," Malcolm said.

"Things I haven't experienced for a long time. Since my wife went away, it has just been me and my son."

"What happened to her, Malcolm?"

"I guess time just took its toll on us. She started traveling with friends and decided not to come back. I still love her, but just not in the same way I once did."

Looking at Malcolm, Kate could see the emptiness in his soul. For the first time, she saw him in a different light as someone to whom she also was becoming attracted. She knew she shouldn't be having these thoughts, not when she was involved with someone else. She couldn't help herself though. The feelings were there. What was she going to do with them? She had a stirring within her now that she wanted to act on, but didn't know how to go about expressing it. She wanted to kiss Malcolm and knew how insane this thought was. He was still married and she engaged -to- be. What kind of woman would Malcolm think she was? She had to find out if what she felt was true or just a passing fancy.

"Kate, walk with me out to my carriage; there's something I want to show you." As they walked the distance to Malcolm's carriage, they discussed the just completed riding lesson. Malcolm kept encouraging her to keep up with the lessons and not give up. Upon arriving at the carriage, Malcolm began to show her a publication he had come across recently when, without warning, Kate reached over to him, grabbed his face in her hands, and kissed him very passionately on the lips for several seconds. As she did so, Malcolm held the kiss with her and enjoyed the moment. As she broke the kiss, a look of astonishment came over her and she looked as if she were going to faint.

"Kate, it's okay, don't panic." Malcolm tried to calm her and bring her back to reality. Malcolm was pleased with the surprise kiss, and so was she as she made her apology to Malcolm for her sudden expression of affection: "It'll be alright, please don't worry. I'll see you later. Take care."

Malcolm was elated with what had just taken place. He didn't care that she was engaged and he didn't care who might have seen them together. He was feeling emotions that he had thought were dead. They were not. He was

30

emotionally on the highest mountain . What a great day this had turned out to be. He wanted Kate to be alright with what had happened.

"I will try and see you tomorrow. Good-bye," Kate said. Kate climbed aboard her carriage and headed down the road to her home. Malcolm walked back to the barn the happiest he had been in longer than he could remember. What a sudden turn of developments, he thought.Things that he didn't expect to happen became a surprise reality. How was he going to get through the rest of the day? There was no way he could concentrate on anything else at the moment. He only had thoughts of her and what had just taken place. He decided to take the rest of the day off to relax and think. He needed to think about the rest of his life and where he had been for so many years in his rut of a life. He loved his work, but now a new outlook on life was before him. He knew he was on a different path that he hadn't been on in a long time. How could just one kiss cause him to rethink his life? What weight did this kiss hold? Why was this kiss that special? Malcolm knew that he would not sleep well this night.

Seven

"How did that man get loose? You'll take his place if he's not apprehended," said the High Constable.

Daniel had made it out the door, knocking over one guard and pushing aside another as he made his way to freedom and away from the dreaded jail cells. He wasn't home free yet as he had to find a place to hide and then put some distance between himself and the jailers. Unable to believe that anyone could escape from the cells, the guards were completely taken by surprise. As they regained their senses, they started their pursuit of the escapee with all they could muster. Daniel wasn't looking back yet as he made his way into the woods, which he knew very well. He stayed off the well trodden paths and made new ones as he eluded his captors and kept them confused. All the time he had spent in the wilderness was paying off for him now when he needed it.

The jailers were angry about letting Daniel get away. They took inventory of the prisoners to establish who had escaped. After several minutes, they determined it was Daniel MacGow. "Mr. Higginbottom is not going to like this. What do we tell him?"

"I'm not sure, but I think we should try to get him back first. At least if we recapture him, it won't seem so bad," said one of the guards.

"How hard could it be to capture one man on foot when we've got him outnumbered?" asked another of the guard unit.

Daniel had made good time in distancing himself from the angry jailers. He needed to get supplies and make his way out of the territory if he was to survive. He also thought about the other prisoners who might be executed on false charges just so the religious men could keep power. Daniel knew he could make his way to a safe haven at this point, but felt the tug on his heart to lend a helping hand to the outrageous events here in Salem. But what could he do? How could he help these people?Daniel continued to make his way through the woods, cutting his own trails to throw off the pursuing guards. After criss-crossing in the forest for over an hour, Daniel decided to trust a friend that he knew who lived not far from the river overlooking the bay. Angus McPhee had befriended him when he first arrived in the Colonies and made him feel welcome in this new land. Angus was from the western part of Scotland on the isles called the Hebrides. Even though Daniel's family was from the eastern part of Scotland, the two Scots hit it off very well and had been friends ever since.

As Daniel made his way to the cottage of Angus, he could see candles burning through the windows and knew Angus was home. Making sure no one was on the road, Daniel quickly made his way from the wooded area and approached the front door. Taking care not to disturb the beautiful flower bed that the missus had planted, he stepped over the garden flowers and landed on the front porch. He rapped only loud enough to get the attention of Angus and hoped he would come quickly to let him in.

"I'm coming, I'm coming. Just hold on a minute," came the voice of Angus. Hearing the latch move and seeing the door swing widely open, Daniel saw Angus McPhee, standing there with a startled look on his face as if he had seen a haunt.

"Well, you going to let me come in or not?"

Regaining his composure, Angus remarked, "Get in here and close the door. Don't you know the jailers are after you?"

"Of course I know. Why do you think I've been hiding in the forest all day? I take it you've heard of my escape."

"I've heard. You're a brave man, Daniel."

"Brave? How about desperate? I'm not ready to hang for any religion, especially one that I don't practice. Why are these people acting this way, Angus? Is this really the way Christ wants his people to behave?"

"No, I don't think it is. It wasn't always this way, at least not from what I recollect from when I first arrived. There seem to be other forces at work in this colony. People used to get along and were not so judgmental toward each other. It seems as if they're interpreting scripture in a literal manner and making everyone miserable in the process. These same Puritans that came here because of religious persecution are now persecuting each other and whoever doesn't fit their brand of Bible understanding."

"You know, I can hide very well in the woods just east of here and they would never find me, but I didn't come this far to start over again. I've built a life here and want to get back to it. I can't fight them alone. What do you suggest, Angus?"

Angus, stroking his long beard and looking for the right words to say, looked at Daniel and walked toward the mantle of his fireplace to light his pipe. "Daniel, we can't fight them with guns, and they have the law on their side. I would suggest that we form a citizens committee and try to sway public opinion. The problem is we may be arrested for defending the Devil's work or some such charge." Angus struck a match and puffed his pipe until it was lit. With a cloud of smoke around his face, he said to Daniel, "I know a few friends who are also fed up with the deeds of these zealots and would be happy to have the whole affair over with so we can get some normalcy here again. One of them is a little strange but a good person nonetheless. As a matter of fact, he arrived about the same time as you did last year. He is trustworthy though. If I can arrange a meeting, you'll get to see him."

"What do you suggest I do in the meantime? I don't want to put you and your wife at risk."

"Martha is at her sister's for a visit so she is safe there. As for me, I don't fear them that can kill the body. You are welcome to stay here. I have a trap door in the bedroom if unwanted visitors should arrive."

As Angus tried to reassure Daniel that things would work out, he thought of his own past back in Scotland. Where he was from, out on the islands of western Scotland, he were left pretty much alone. A few clan feuds erupted now and then, but peace eventually reigned and life went on. Living on an island did have its advantages. Angus's people had migrated to the isles years ago and stayed among people who were not naturally their own families but were eventually accepted. His heart thought back to those times and the people he loved and missed there.

"I appreciate your hospitality, Angus, and I'll try not to be a burden. At the first sign of real trouble, I'll head for the woods and not return. Right now I'd like to rest. I haven't slept for awhile, and I'm too tired to even think straight."

"I'll make you a bedroll, and you can nap in the back storage area where we can stack up supplies to hide you."

"I thank you again, Angus. I'll never forget your kind helping hand."

"How could you let him escape? I thought you were better than that! I've a trial to attend at the moment, and I expect you to find one Daniel MacGow and bring him back alive for trial. Is that understood?" said the furious and red-faced Theodore Higginbottom.

"Yes, your excellency. We shall not rest until he is captured," said the captain of the guard. The pressure from Higginbottom put all of the guard unit in an emotional vise. Why, they thought, was this accused one so important? What made him a top priority to Theodore Higginbottom anyway? Those men of the special unit did not have the answer but they surely had a mission at which they could not fail. They had never encountered any trouble from the accused witches until Daniel came along, because most of the accused were older women who could not put up a fight. The guards thought it funny that it was almost always old women that stood trial. There was the occasional older man, like the one that Higginbottom was now going to prosecute, but they were few and far between.

"Your honor, before you stands George Jacobs. He is accused of cavorting with known witches that were convicted right in this very same court, Your Honor. He has bewitched these young girls to the point that they voice gibberish and fall to the floor as if drunk."

"Thank you, Mr. Higginbottom," said Judge John Hathorne. "You sir, George Jacobs, how do you plead to the charges?"

"I have done no wrong, Your Honor. I go about my business and do no harm to anyone. Please release me, I pray."

"We will see what the evidence produces first, Mr. Jacobs. Mr. Higginbottom, state your case please."

Higginbottom began. "These witches have corrupted innocent girls—girls who have not even had the time to finish school and learn the ways of womanhood or become the wife of one of our fine citizens—and who have now been bewitched by devilish devices with card games and trickery."

One of the girls stood and began to dance around the court, twirling faster and faster and making strange sounds before she fell to the floor and began writhing. The court and its audience gasped in horror at the sight. The other girls began to laugh and snicker upon seeing their friend go through such gyrations. They too went into a form of possession as the men and women in attendance became agitated and had to be restrained by the court deputies. They wanted the accused to hang for what they perceived as a horrible deed

36

done to their children. "Your Honor, please, I have no control of these young ones. I have done them or no one else any wrong deed. Please believe me," spoke George Jacobs in his defense.

Mr. Higginbottom spoke up with anger and disdain and said, "Your Honor, now you can see for yourself the spells he has exposed these innocent children to and the resulting harm they have incurred. I say we have a duty to preserve our society and rid ourselves of this plague upon the good people of Salem Village before its too late for the rest of us. I believe the prosecution has proven its case and justice demands swift punishment for the likes as such of these. The prosecution rests."

"Based upon the evidence presented in this court this August 18th 1692, I decree that Mr. George Jacobs, Sr., along with the other defendants who previously have been found guilty of witchcraft offenses, be hanged by the neck until dead on the morrow, August 19th 1692, at Gallows Hill. God's will is done this day. Amen."

And so it went. On August 19th 1692, George Jacobs and several other innocent victims were hanged on Gallows Hill for crimes of witchcraft. Judge John Hathorne along with Jonathan Corwin, his assistant, had passed their judgment on these Salem Village folk. The purge continued. Unbeknownst to the crowd that followed the procession, there were three men who were taking special interest in the hangings and the court processions. They remained quiet and stayed out of sight for the most part but were very much involved. They were taking note of who did what to whom and the attitudes of those involved. They dressed differently from most of the town folk and were never together but stayed to themselves, yet they acted as one unit. They seemed to communicate with one another without speaking. Mysterious was one way of describing them, but they presented no threat. Angelic would be another way to describe them. The graves were dug and the bodies placed within them; in a most rude and unfeeling way, they were quickly covered up with the fresh dirt that came from the hole. No words were spoken over them nor were there any markers to identify the person buried there. As quickly as the crowd arrived, they left. Some came along to see if by chance the bodies might rise from those same graves. By this time, the three men who had been watching had already gone too.

Daniel had slept through the latter part of the day and all through the night without waking and was surprised that the time had gotten away from him. "Angus, why didn't you wake me? I didn't mean to overstay my time here and take advantage of your hospitality."

"You looked like you needed the rest. Besides, you were well out of sight. I must admit though, your snoring might have been a dead giveaway," Angus laughed out loud. "If you could have seen your face when you arrived yesterday, you'd see why I let you sleep. You looked like death warmed over."

"I have to admit it was a trying experience being in that dark, damp jail cell. It put a mighty hard strain on me to say the least."

"As I was tending to the morning chores outside, things looked normal to me. No sign of soldiers or any strangers passing by. That's certainly a good sign," Angus said.

"Quiet, maybe too quiet, Angus. I'm going to try and make it to my home. There are some things there that I need so I'll be able to survive in the wilderness if it comes to that; my weapons and extra food supply could make the difference between life and death for me."

Daniel had become very self sufficient and was able to fend for himself, having traversed the wilderness in his fur trade business. He found that the ones they called savages had more civility than those who pursued him for reasons he was not even guilty of. It seemed to Daniel that some sort of system of justice should be installed to protect the innocent from false accusations. Maybe in the future that would be the case. It certainly wasn't now though. Running for his life for no reason was so appalling to Daniel that it made his Scottish blood boil. Oh well, he thought to himself, this is the hand I have been dealt and play it to the end I will.

Daniel was aware that Angus was getting up in years, at least in comparison to himself. Angus wasn't feeble or anything like that, but he did move slower than Daniel, and Daniel didn't want any harm to come to him. He knew he had to leave now and hoped his stay here wouldn't come back to haunt Angus.

"Angus, I want to thank you once more for your hospitality, but I must be moving on now. You have been a real friend to me and a life- saver."

"Please, Daniel, feel free to stay as long as you wish. I'll make us some rabbit stew with all the fixings, and we'll dine like kings."

"Angus, you've done more than enough for me. I couldn't have asked for a better host. Besides, your wife will be coming home soon, and you all need to get back to a normal way of life here. I would eventually be seen by someone, even by mistake, and you know how people talk. No, it's best that I move on. I have a lot of work to do, and I need the freedom to do it."

As Daniel packed up the supplies that Angus had prepared for him, the thought came to him that trouble and torment would catch up to a person no matter where he went or what he was doing. Daniel hadn't regretted coming to this new country or even the hardships that his new line of work often brought him. His frustration stemmed from the unnecessary dealings which had to be confronted that weren't his concern. He now knew though, that the plight of other people could draw him in and make it his fight as well. As independent as Daniel wanted to be, he could no longer think solely of himself. This was a hard lesson that he was learning, but it was a part of his maturing and something he now had to embrace, not only for the sake of others, but for himself as well.

Eight

Malcolm wasn't sleeping too well these days. With all the unexpected events that were taking place around him, he had never been this disheveled in his whole life. With the news of his long time friend Alasdair Downie murdered just last night, and the news of his brother Daniel possibly being in danger in America, he was really beside himself. The only good to come to him lately was the new relationship he had been propelled into with Kate MacPherson, with whom he was fast becoming enamored. She was someone who he thought was sent into his life in his time of need. She was practically perfect. Oh, she had her quirks, but didn't everybody? He knew he had his, but these were things that people just had to accept in and go on. Malcolm thought she was the most beautiful woman he had ever seen and told her so every chance he got. He just hoped she wouldn't think he was just saying that for ulterior purposes, because he wasn't. She brought out the praise in him for her so easily that he hoped she wouldn't get sick of how he practically swooned over her all the time. The morning came for Malcolm. Being the first in the kitchen, he quickly prepared a simple breakfast of scones and tea. He knew Ian would probably make a platter of scotch eggs and bridies for his breakfast, but he wanted to get started working as soon as possible. He enjoyed firing up the forge and feeling the power that emanated from it each day. That same power seemed to flow into Malcolm as he beat the iron into the designs and shapes for the day's orders. Clansmen in the area always wanted to have a premier sword to show off to their colleagues and with which to make their first kill in battle. They knew that Malcolm was a great sword maker and could also wield it as well as any of their warriors. He had taught many of them the art of warfare, both offensive and defensive tactics. Although he seldom took part in battle anymore, he would, on occasion, accompany the troop to the field to survey the battlements. Malcolm's kilt seemed to always be grimier than the rest, probably because of the work he did at the forge. Lots of soot and smoke flew through the air and coated everything in sight. Although he wore an apron over his kilt to prevent sparks from igniting it, it still looked rather soiled most of the time.

Ian had finally awakened and did exactly what his father thought he would do: he made enough food for two people to eat, except Ian was eating it all by himself. Ian could put it away, but where, Malcolm could not figure out. Ian had grown nearly as big as his father and had taken on the characteristics of Malcolm with a lean, hard, muscular body that was very athletic and strong from working the iron every day. Ian would sometimes compete in the local games with other sons of clansmen and do quite well, considering some of them were much bigger and stronger than Ian. He was well liked, and they knew they had to be at their best to beat Ian.

After breakfast, Ian joined his father at the forge to start the day's work and to try to improve his speed at completing his tasks. He made it a personal competition to better himself each day.

"Good morning, son. Decided to come to work today I see."

"I figured you couldn't handle it by yourself, considering your age and all," Ian quipped. "Besides, I need to set a new record for myself today and make that sword for John Duncan. He brags that he can wield a sword bigger than Wallace himself did, and I want to prove him wrong. He has paid me half already and will pay the rest when I deliver the sword. I figure that in another six days I'll have it ready for the big fellow."

"I'm glad he paid you something in advance. We don't want to waste our time and energy on nonsense for a braggart," Malcolm said. "Oh, I'm smarter than that, Dad. Besides, I want to be there when he shows off to the rest of the gang and looks foolish with something he can't handle. I'll probably earn a few more pounds when I have to cut it down to something he can actually handle," Ian laughed.

"John is a big man, you know. He just might be able to throw it around somewhat. You know what he can do at the games. I remember last summer when he heaved the stone at least six feet farther than the best throw of the day. I wouldn't sell him short, Ian."

"I'm not. It's just that he's such a show-off and likes to flaunt himself all the time."

"Well, you just do the good quality work like I've taught you and we'll see how big John holds out. Okay?"

"Sounds fine to me. Hey, there seems to be more people out and about this morning than usual. I wonder what's going on?"

"You're right. Hey, Jamie . . . Jamie Blackburn," Malcolm called out. "What's all the commotion about this early morning hour?"

"They found a man dead earlier this day. The constables said he was dressed rather strangely and had a note pinned to his cloak," Jamie said.

"Anyone we might know?" Malcolm asked.

"Don't think so. He doesn't look like he's from anywhere near these parts. They took him to the Tolbooth for further investigation." Malcolm couldn't believe that still another odd thing had taken place in such a short span of time. Malcolm suddenly remembered what the pastor had said to him that he was being watched and was in danger from those who hold a grudge. Malcolm got cold chills just from that very thought as this whole thing grew closer to him and Ian. It was a kind of fear, not of facing a man in combat— Malcolm had done that on many occasions– but this fear was from an unseen hand that moved in on its prey without notice. As far as Malcolm knew, it was something that he couldn't see coming and he didn't know when it would come— something that might give no warning before killing him and then vanishing. This was an enemy unlike any that Malcolm had ever faced previously. "I've got to know what that note said. This concerns me and my son. I've a right to have all the facts I can get. Thanks, Jamie, thanks for the information."

As Jamie went about his business, he wondered what Malcolm meant by it being his concern. "Oh well," he said to himself, "no reason to get too worried about a drifter coming through town. He probably had made enemies by cheating them somehow. Probably got what he deserved."

"Ian, I've got to go get to the bottom of this latest killing. I want you to stay here, but be on guard . Keep an extra eye out around here for anyone who looks like they don't belong in these parts. Also, keep your personal sword handy and your black knife in your boot, just in case. We're obviously involved and I don't know why as yet, but I will. Do we understand each other?"

"Aye, Dad. I'll be all right. You just watch out for yourself."As Malcolm made his way to the Tolbooth at High and Castle Streets, he couldn't help but hear the clamor of fear in the voices of those he passed by. He only caught parts of conversations as he walked the streets to his destination, but putting them all together, he thought they spelled concern for the tiny community and gave him the feeling that the outside world had touched Forfar for the worst. Malcolm thought about the guided tour he had given to the investors and wondered if he had done the right thing in wanting the area to expand to bring more trade into the market scene. If this was an example of what was to come, then maybe he had made a mistake. Maybe it would be best to remain an isolated village where everyone knew each other and the community maintained a sense of togetherness as they moved slowly through time. After all, their fathers had never complained about new roads or having a bigger base to deal in business. Maybe they should count their blessings and be content to live out their lives as their fathers before them had. Malcolm was seeing the possible down side of his quest to move into the eighteenth century. It was becoming a confusing world for Malcolm.

As he neared the Tolbooth, Malcolm caught the scent of fresh fish in the open market in town and saw even more people milling about doing their shopping. Being near the coast, a town like Forfar could have the pleasure of a new menu of fish each day as soon as the boats came back in from their overnight trips out to sea. Meat was another market item that Forfar relished, as Highland cattle was a staple to the Scottish diet. Malcolm, seeing the cross that sat on the main crossroads of the village, received a sense of courage to face this battle that was before him. The market was abuzz with the news of the body of the man that had been brought in early that morning. Malcolm would see people huddled together to guard their conversations from those they didn't want overhearing them. Others spoke openly, not caring who would hear them stating their opinions. Malcolm knew he had to guard his own words, considering his possible involvement in this whole affair.

Upon reaching his destination, the Tolbooth, Malcolm announced his presence and asked to be seen by the magistrate.

"Malcolm, good to see you, lad. Do come in and make yourself comfortable," spoke Mr. David Falconer, the current magistrate. As Malcolm made his way into the inner office and then to the office of the magistrate, he couldn't help but notice lavish decor and style. A desk that appeared to be mahogany was covered with piles of papers in neat stacks. Everything was in perfect order and symmetry. The windows looked to have been recently washed to the point of sparkling with no fingerprints or smudges on the panes. A hall tree sat against the back wall and had only one garment hanging on it, which Malcolm guessed belonged to Mr. Falconer. Malcolm surmised that not too many prisoners or that ilk ever made it to stand in front of the magistrate in this office. He used

5

it only for preferred guests by invitation and made sure that any low-life would be dealt with in another chamber in the big stone building. No one was going to make a mess of this opulent showroom.

"Mr. MacGow, won't you please be seated."

Malcolm made his way to the big stuffed chair in front of the polished wooden desk and slowly descended into its rich, thick cushion.

"You act like you were expecting me or something. Has this to do with the murder?"

"It has everything to do with the murder. You may not know it, but Pastor Bruce already paid me a visit this morning on your behalf. He said you and probably Ian were possible targets of a person or persons who have it in for you. He was only looking out for your safety, Malcolm. He sounded very concerned."

"Well, can you tell me who the man is that was killed and what it has to do with me?"

"We've never seen him before, but Pastor Bruce has. The man had talked to the pastor just last night. Malcolm, I don't want this next question to appear accusatory, but I have to ask it anyway. Do you have any connection to... well...?"

"To what, Magistrate, any connection to what?"

"To witchcraft or witches?" the magistrate asked.

"Of course not. Who started that rumor?"

"The note that was pinned to the cloak of the deceased made reference to the fact that someone was associated with witchcraft in some capacity."

"Druids . . .," Malcolm said with a distant look as though thinking back to the past history of his family. "This someone is confusing witchcraft with Druids. They think my family are witches. My father was accused many years ago by this same group who started a witch frenzy some thirty years back. My father had to defend himself against them and actually killed a man over this charge. I can't believe they're still active after all this time. What drives them to keep this madness up?"

"Would . . . you like to see what the note said?" the magistrate asked. "It's right here in my desk, let me get it." The magistrate went right to the drawer that contained the note and pulled it out. Straightening the creases to make it more readable, he handed it to Malcolm. As Malcolm took it in his hands, he focused his eyes on the writing and began to read, "YOUR KIND WILL NOT SURVIVE – WE HAVE HUNTED YOU FOR OVER A THOUSAND YEARS – WE WILL NOT REST UNTIL YOU EXIST NO MORE.

MORS VENEFICIS"

"This is obviously an organized group that has an agenda," Malcolm commented. "Magistrate, may I see the body?"

"I don't see why not. Please, come with me. We have him in the basement where it's cooler." Leaving the office they met with the constable on duty, Constable Ogilvie. "Please lead the way to the basement rooms, Mr. Ogilvie."

Making their way down the hallway to the entrance to the basement, Malcolm noticed that the view began to change for the worse as the light became dimmer and an unpleasant odor made him gag. Down the wide stone steps the three descended as they came to the bottom into an open room that had many doors. Some of the doors were actually jail cells and Malcolm really didn't want to know about the rest of them.

"This way," Constable Ogilvie said as they came to a double door that he swung open to accommodate the group. "We have him on the table over here." As they approached the table, they took up different positions around the body as the constable pulled back the sheet so Malcolm could view the body.

"I do not know him," Malcolm said, "but there is something I can tell you about him. He is a Druid priest. I remember them from when I was a boy. They would visit my father, Robert, and we would go to the groves where they performed their ceremonies. I didn't really understand what was taking place then, but my father did explain some of the rituals to me as I grew older. The Druids were good people and loved my father very much. He had a certain connection with them. I believe it had something to do with the history of blacksmiths and an ancient bond that existed a long way back. I really don't know much more than that. Wish I could be more helpful."

"You've been very helpful, Malcolm. This is more than we knew earlier and maybe we can piece things together and find the killer," the magistrate said.

"Or *killers*," Malcolm added. "I've a feeling that more than just one person is carrying this out. It would appear that I've inherited my father's problem, and it's being passed from one generation to another. These same people have also killed my longtime friend, Alasdair Downie, up in the Strathmore area. I'm not going to back down from this. If it's a fight they want, it's a fight they'll get."

"You need to remain calm, Malcolm. Let me and my office track these men down. We'll bring them to a swift justice. Just go home, protect yourselves, but let us handle this," Magistrate Falconer said. "I've no desire to do your job, sir, but I'm not going to become a target either. By the way, Magistrate, how did the Druid die?"

"He was found hanging from an oak tree. What was funny though is that it was the only oak tree in that area while there were plenty of other big trees to have hanged him from. It's like they went out of their way to hang him from a tree that took a lot of extra effort to get to."

"You said oak tree. I know why they picked that tree. The oak is considered sacred and is associated with nature and wisdom in the Druid religion. They hanged him there as a sort of mockery to his faith."

"I see," said Magistrate Falconer. "They apparently have some knowledge of the Druids' ways themselves. What we do not have is information and knowledge of these killers and their organization, but I assure you, we will."

"Please keep me informed of your progress, Magistrate, and I would appreciate any protection you could give us. I'm not so concerned about myself, but about my son, Ian."

"We will come by every chance we get, but you must understand: this is a burgh that has only four officers, and they do have to sleep sometime. We will stay as close as we can though."

Malcolm continued to work as always at his blacksmithing while keeping an eye out for Ian at all times. Nothing unusual had occurred for the past few days, but still Malcolm wasn't dropping his guard to provide an opening for an enemy that he knew was still lurking about. He knew that this was the day that Kate MacPherson would be coming by for her session of horseback riding lessons. He needed a calmness in his life with all the stress that had taken place recently. Kate made him feel alive on the inside, and she was such a welcome diversion from his everyday routine. Malcolm also knew something else that he hadn't shared with anyone; he was in love with Kate. He hadn't told her yet but knew he had to and probably should today. He would wait for the right time. He didn't know how it happened, because he had not planned to fall in love. He had not even been looking in that emotional direction, but nevertheless, it happened. He thought about her at varying times throughout the day, about the times they went for carriage rides in the countryside and had a picnic or when they would just sit somewhere and talk about their lives and how they arrived at this point in time. They shared everything that came to mind, even very personal things that they had not shared with anyone else in their lives. Malcolm knew things about Kate that even her fiancé did not know. They were so at ease with each other that it was as if they already knew what the other was going to say.

"Ian, my trainee is here for her lesson. Will you watch the forge and keep an eye on things?" Ian knew what his father was talking about when he asked him to keep an eye on things. He knew he was to watch for any unusual people or conditions which might signal some sort of attack on them. Ian was very watchful and was going to make a great warrior in time. He had cat-like reflexes and a strong arm to wield a sword. The forge was situated in such a manner that Ian or Malcolm faced the open double doors of the barn area so that they could see anyone walking up. The back of the barn was enclosed and fortified with strong heavy wooden boards that would take a minor explosive to penetrate. Working in a forge was noisy and hot, and sometimes it was hard to talk and work at the same time.

"Kate, so good to see you once more," Malcolm said.

"Hello, it's good to see you again too, Malcolm."

"Are you ready to get started?" Malcolm asked.

"I am. Can you show me something different today? I want to learn all I can about controlling the horse. If you don't mind, I'd like to stretch first if I could. I was really sore and stiff after our last lesson for some reason."

"Sure, go ahead and take your time. When you feel ready, we'll start," Malcolm said. Kate didn't take that long and was now ready tobegin. As Malcolm took her through several exercises on the horse, she would catch him just staring at her with a slight smile on his face. "What are you staring at?" she asked.

"Just you. Forgive me. I can't help it. Go on with the exercise," Malcolm said. At some point in the exercise, it became necessary for Malcolm to take her reins to guide her in the right direction through a movement she wasn't getting quite right. At those moments, he would purposely touch her hand and fingers and allow his hand to linger for a while in that position. Kate knew exactly what he was doing, but played along with the gesture because she too enjoyed his touch. She was feeling the exact same thing in her heart. Malcolm and Kate were becoming one as they spent more and more time with one another. Malcolm could not contain himself at times and would practically embarrass Kate with his schoolboy antics. He was almost giddy with excitement, and his eyes were bright and wide open with just the presence of Kate next to him. Kate was basically the same way. Her face naturally lit up any area she was in. Her smile was big, the light just radiating from her.

After about an hour session of horse training, Kate was getting tired and wanted to stop for the day.

"Okay, do you want to train again in a few days?"

"Yes, I do. I'll let you know the time," Kate said.

"Could I see you before then, I mean, if you want to?" Malcolm asked.

"Yes, I'd like that. I know a place where we can talk if you'd like. It's down the dead-end road that curves around to the glen. Do you know the road I'm talking about?" Kate asked.

Kate explained the directions to the road, and Malcolm finally understood. At around noon the following day, Malcolm had no trouble locating the place. Actually, Kate met him halfway to guide him just in case. As they neared the end of the road, they pulled their carriages alongside each other. They dismounted and walked toward each other and quickly embraced upon reaching one another. Their lips met and held a deep kiss for longer than usual as they enjoyed every moment of their passion for each other.

"You know, Kate, I've never in my life had a kiss from anyone who kissed the way you do. I must admit I have had quite a few, but nothing compares with yours," Malcolm said with sincere passion. "I'm not just reciprocating your same thoughts, but it's true of your kisses too. I must confess something else to you since we've shared so much already; I can't stand kissing my fiancé at all. I know it sounds awful and I do care for him, but just not his kisses."

"Seems we're on the same path with this subject. I just can't believe how good you feel when I hold you and kiss you," Malcolm said. "Kate, there's something I have to tell you as well. I don't say what I'm about to say to you lightly, but I am sincere when I say it."

"What is it, Malcolm?"

"Kate, I love you!" Malcolm was looking into Kate's eyes when he said it, and she said nothing at first. She looked down, fumbling with her buttons in a nervous sort of way before finally looking back up to Malcolm. She kissed him again and they embraced once more with a hug that said 'I'm never letting go.'

"I love you so much, Kate, and I've never felt this kind of love before," Malcolm said. "I want to spend the rest of my life with you." Kate didn't know what to say. She was amazed that she had affected Malcolm to this degree.

"You are so sweet, and I care very much for you too," Kate responded. "Your presence does wonders for me. I feel so good when I'm with you. I don't ever want it to end."

Kate and Malcolm always had a hard time saying good-bye. They knew they would see each other again very soon, but they just didn't want to break the moment. After finally saying their last good-bye for the day, Kate went her way and Malcolm did the same. Of course, they had already made their next date and were counting down the hours.

Nine

Daniel had no problem making his way through the wooded area as he was adept at such travel. He was well rested and had enough supplies to last several days if need be, thanks to a Mr. Angus McPhee. Daniel was glad to be away from him so as not to bring any grief upon him and his house. As Daniel was making his way to his own cottage, he had the feeling that he wasn't alone anymore. He thought about how he had developed a kind of sixth sense to help him when he was out and about on his woodland adventures. It just came naturally as a way of survival. He hadn't needed it in the towns he was from or in the work he used to do, but here in the wilderness where one mistake could be fatal, he was glad to have acquired it.

"Okay, who are you and where are you?" Daniel spoke softly to himself. "I know you're out there watching me, tracking me— for what purpose?" His eyes scanned the horizon and then focused on a closer distance, looking at every tree and hillside to determine where the lurker might be. All of a sudden, Daniel felt as if they were all around him. He decided to hunker down behind a small mound of earth, which had plenty of downed trees for cover to wait and watch for movement he could react to. The silence was starting to play tricks on him as he started to imagine an enemy he hadn't seen as yet. He cleared his mind and focused once more on his own senses to help him through this moment. As he controlled his breathing, his heart also slowed to a more normal sound in his chest, even though his mind was racing with great expectation of what might be out there. There! Over to his left– a shadowy figure just stepped behind a tree. At least he thought he saw that. "I'm sure I saw someone. Over there!" To his right another figure, unusually dressed.

"Okay, I know I saw someone that time," Daniel said to himself. "Who are these . . . peop . . ."

"Daniel! Stay your hand and remain calm; we wish you no harm," came a voice from behind Daniel. "You won't need your weapon."Daniel quickly turned, pointing his pistol at the voice behind him. Shaking noticeably, the gun barrel could not have remained on a straight line to fire if he had desired to do so. Daniel stared at the cloaked figure before him and could not move. It was as if he was paralyzed, unable to move a muscle.

"We are here to help you, Daniel MacGow. We are well aware of your plight concerning your capture and escape from Theodore Higginbottom's prison. We are aware of far more than that."

As the other two companions joined the first one, Daniel had regained his composure and had lowered his weapon. As he stood, still moving very cautiously, he had a feeling of being in the presence of people who were in control in more ways than just sheer numbers. They had an air of authority about them, but in a way that Daniel could not fathom. They seemed to be powerful, but holy. "How could that be?" he thought to himself.

"We have much to discuss, Daniel. Please follow us and you'll learn more about yourself than you thought you ever would," said the first man. "We have a cave just several miles from here where you'll be safe from your pursuers."

Daniel arose to his feet and secured his weapon while dusting his clothes to rid them of the forest debris. It was hard for him not to stare at the cloaked figures as they moved through the woods in an almost silent manner. "What powers do these men possess and who are they that they have business with me?" Daniel said to himself. "I'll go with them for now since I have no better plan available to me. I'll keep my pistol handy just in case— just in case of what? I've a feeling that I'm no match for them, so it probably won't make any difference." They cautiously made their way through the woods, first the original man, then Daniel, and finally the other two. They showed no weapons that he could see, but he knew that they had some form of protection on them somewhere. They were an awesome group of men who evoked power and strength just by their presence. For some strange reason, they gave the impression of being more than just three men.

"We've arrived," said the first man. The entrance to the cave was behind a stand of rhododendron that they separated to make room for them to proceed. It was remarkable how this thick plant hid so much.As they made their way inside, Daniel could see the cave opening up to a bigger cavern as the torchlight illuminated the chamber. They had made it a cozy place to stay with what looked like odds and ends that they had collected from various sources. It wasn't bad for a cave, Daniel thought. There was an open area near the back wall which appeared to be a place where ritualistic practices had taken place. Candles were burning, and a circle of stones had been placed to form some sort of design that made no sense to Daniel. There were some animal skins on one of the walls and what looked like a store of food placed in a hole in the cave floor.

"At least they're eating well," Daniel thought to himself. Of all the different objects scattered around the cave room, the one thing Daniel didn't see were books or any kind of reading materials. He thought this rather odd. These men all carried walking or hiking sticks with them at all times. They were elaborately decorated, almost as if an artist had carved a great piece of art with intrinsically ornate designs. He thought them to be very beautiful.

"Please be seated, Daniel. Make yourself comfortable, at least as well as you can in a cave," the first man spoke. "We have much to talk about with you and want you to be at peace here. You have no need to worry." Daniel was feeling a little better and did feel safe in spite of the fact that he didn't know who they were.

"I suppose that introductions are in order," spoke the first man. "My name is Adam MacGalloglass. I am the highest rank of our order while Richard and Charles are my understudies."

As Adam spoke, Richard was preparing food. Charles had returned the way they had come and was doing a check on their security in the hidden cave."Our food may not be what you are used to, but it will nourish you and make you strong," said Adam. "With the knowledge we possess, we are well able to provide garnishes to improve even this country's diet. I know you have many questions, and I promise you they will all be answered tonight. Be patient."

Richard was very busy in the preparation of the night's meal and worked like it was his only duty in life. He was very adept at what he did. Charles had returned and nodded to Adam in a slow head tilt, as if that was all he needed to do to communicate. Apparently it was, as Adam nodded back in the same fashion.

"Well, it seems we are secure for another night and we should haveno interruptions this evening. It is necessary, Daniel, to conduct our affairs in as much secrecy as we can. Those out there are not able to receive our message or understand our ways. We are from the 'old world' and our customs and ways of conduct belong to those who have gone on before us many eons ago. We are in this colony because of an obligation to your family in Scotland. Do you understand of what I speak, Daniel?"

"My father mentioned on occasion, a group of people who were somewhat mysterious, but I never paid much attention."

"Well, Daniel, it is time you know who we are and why we are here," said Adam. "But before we talk, we eat. Richard is ready to serve us, I believe."

As Daniel took his place near the stone circles and sat cross-legged, he noticed that Charles had no place to sit. "Charles, please sit here by me. There's plenty of room."

"No, Daniel. Charles knows his place and will serve us and then eat later. It is his honor to do nothing else," Adam said. "He is not insulted, for this is our way."

"Okay, I understand," Daniel replied. "What is it we're having, if I may ask?"

"It is what they call turkey. It is a bird that seems to be abundant in these colonies. It takes a long time to prepare, but is well worth the effort in the end," Adam said. After their meal, Charles took care of the clean-up and prepared his own meal. He went about his tasks without complaining and never changed his expression. Candles were lit throughout the cave which provided plenty of light to illuminate the entire room. Daniel noticed that there were bedding supplies on one side of the cave, where apparently the men slept. Daniel figured that he too would occupy one of those spots tonight. Adam made himself comfortable and asked Daniel to do the same. "Daniel, I hope you have enjoyed our hospitality tonight."

"Your food was very good, Adam. It seems cave life suits you well. I still would not want to make this my permanent home though," Daniel said.

"We too are not cave dwellers. We prefer the daylight with the sun and the moon at night. This place is practical for the moment. When enemies are made, it is sometimes best to stay out of sight, whichbrings us to the 'why' of this conversation. Our reason for being in this country is to protect you, Daniel— a mission that started long ago in Scotland. Daniel, have you not heard of the Druids?" Adam continued.

"That's it! You're Druids! I should have guessed sooner— the robes and the way you conduct yourselves. You have powers and abilities that make you invincible, I've heard. You are Druids, right?"

"Yes, Daniel, we are Druids. We are not invincible though. That is an exaggeration. We do have powers that have been developed over many years and abilities that have taken us twenty years or more to learn. This cave for instance— had never before been occupied by anyone human until we found it. It was our ability to hone it to a place of refuge in a time of need that led us to it. We are quite safe here since no one but us knows it exists," Adam said.

"Amazing, simply amazing! You mentioned a mission. How does that concern me?" Daniel asked.

"It concerns you, your brother, and his son also. It started with your father, Robert, back in Scotland," Adam remarked.

As Daniel made himself comfortable, he noticed how Richard was busy finishing his dinner and Charles was sitting very quietly as if contemplating the day's activities, or maybe tomorrow's. They never interrupted Adam, but knew their places and were content in them. "By the way, Daniel, you would have never made it to your cottage. The powers that be have occupied your quarters days ago, and you would have walked into a trap. Higginbottom has left no stone unturned to get you back. He figured you would eventually try to return there. We too are watching Mr. Higginbottom just to stay ahead of him when we can. He is an evil man to say the least," Adam said. "Back to why we're all here together. Your father grew up with the knowledge of the Druids simply because his father was a full Druid. He was a Druid blacksmith to be exact. Although weapons making was kept to a minimum, he still used his skills to make other implements that our village needed. Your grandfather was a very skilled blacksmith and also an excellent Druid priest. He possessed great knowledge which he learned from frequent trips to Chartres in France.

Although most of the Druid influence and power has long since died away, there are still wise sages there that have great and important knowledge that they pass on to new Druids," Adam said with a coarse and strained voice. "I need just a little of your wine, Richard, for my dry throat." Richard responded immediately to the need of Adam and came with a flask of wine that he poured into Adam's mout to minister to him. Daniel marveled at the way they would help one another and work as a single unit to achieve their purposes. They truly knew their place in service to their religion.

"Pardon the interruption, Daniel, but as I get older, my body seems to require more attention," Adam said.

"I understand, sir."

"Where was I? Oh, yes. Your grandfather earned his way by completing all the tasks set forth by the Arch-Druid in his day. He had the potential to be a great Druid leader in time. These same attributes were passed on to your father, but he just wasn't as interested in walking that path. He was more involved in Christianity and felt that was his calling. Your brother Malcolm did learn quite a bit about the Druid practice though before abandoning it for his own religion. Your father earned the respect of the Druid sect near Forfar one year when he became involved with the intervention of a young Druid apprentice whom Joel Higginbottom, son of Theodore Higginbottom, had tried to arrest on suspicion of being a witch. Your father, Robert, was tutoring this young lad at a grove near his farm when Joel sprang from the woods to accuse them both of being witches. Your father tried to explain that they were not witches but rather Druids. Joel would have no part of it. He wanted to add to the body count to impress his father and make a name for himself. Robert tried everything he could to convince Joel that he had made a mistake in his accusation, but still Joel would not listen. Joel attempted to arrest the boy first. That's when Robert struck Joel, knocking him to the ground. Joel was infuriated and challenged Robert to a duel," Adam spoke and paused. "I never knew what happened to my father when he died. Do you also know the answer to this?" Daniel asked.

"That I do, Daniel. When it came time for the duel, Robert had the option of choosing the weapons since Joel had issued the challenge. Unfortunately for Joel, Robert chose claymores, which he also made and was as skilled with as any highland warrior ever had been. Robert had knocked the sword from Joel's hands three times and had given him the choice of departing back to his home, but Joel refused. Joel was killed as he tried to hack away at Robert.Robert took it hard, but it had to end that way. The young Druid was grateful and sought for a way to pay him back. Your father was killed several months later by poisoning. A form of nightshade was used, probably slipped in his food or drink when he was out with guests or friends. The telltale signs were on his body afterwards. By the way, the young lad whom Robert saved that day . . . was my son," Adam tearfully said.

Ten

Malcolm pondered what he had seen and heard— from the death of the Druid whose body now lay at the Tolbooth and the note fastened to his cloak, to how he had become a target of a fanatical organization. He worried about his son, Ian, and how all of this would impact him. As much of a man as Ian was, Malcolm felt that he was no match for these people of revenge and death.

It was another day that came quickly as Malcolm made himself a pot of coffee. A hot drink was something he needed to get his day started and try and figure out how he would proceed from this time on. He wasn't that hungry and stayed with his coffee as he thought deeply about the whole affair. He thought back to when his father was alive and some of the things he had heard him talk about and the people who visited him. His father had his regular customers that he dealt with, but on occasion he would have men who were not typical customers. It was these men that made Malcolm begin to rack his brain, for he knew they held a possible key to part of this mystery. He figured that they had to be the Druids and that his father had business dealings with them. When he was younger, it never crossed his mind that they were anything other than legitimate clients.

Ian was now getting up and getting ready for a full day's work at the forge. Of course, he would have his usual breakfast of everything he could find to eat. Malcolm always thought it funny that Daniel and his son both inherited a culinary ability and took full advantage of it every day they could. They loved to eat and cook– not that Malcolm was complaining, as he was always near one of them to take advantage of their talent. Malcolm was finishing his coffee when Ian came into the room fixing his kilt and belt buckle.

"Ian, I think you might be outgrowing that kilt you have on," Malcolm said. "Either the wool is shrinking or you're getting bigger– maybe both."

"Ah, this kilt's alright; it's just well broken in," Ian said. "It's got a lot of wear left in it, Dad."

"I think the Widow Macphorich might be enticed to weave you another one if the price is right," Malcolm commented. "She is probably the best kilt maker in these parts and worth every pound you have to pay."

"Well, Dad, if you make the purchase, I will wear it," Ian said. "I didn't say I was buying, but I will put something toward it if you decide to place the order. The threadbare look just doesn't suit you."

"Okay, I'll think about it, but I'm not rushing into it anytime soon," Ian said.

"Just something to think about. You know, Ian, Widow Macphorich comes from Eilean na Peiste, 'the isle of the beast' in the river Don. You don't want to get her riled up if you know what's good for you," Malcolm said.

Ian, laughing, agreed with Malcolm and set about making his hearty breakfast.

After a full day's work, Malcolm was cleaning the forge and tidying up the work area. Ian had already left, for he was running errands to get ready for tomorrow's work. Cooling down the forge to make sure that nothing catches fire was an important part of blacksmithing. There had been a few barns that had burned to the ground from careless housekeeping in nearby forges through the years. Malcolm always made sure that everything was in its place for the next day's work. The sun was low in the western sky and cast shadows throughout the barn and forge. The last of Malcolm's customers had just loaded their wagons and were pulling out as Malcolm heard the clompity-clomp of the horses' hoofs making their way down the road from the forge. As Malcolm was returning his tools to their holding place on the walls, he heard the barn door creak open and then shut. "Sorry, but the forge is closed for the day." Malcolm turned around to face the late customer. He could only make out a cloaked figure, standing very still and facing Malcolm near the doorway. "We'll be open early tomorrow if we can be of service to . . . you," Malcolm said in a slow and alarmed voice. "Do I know you, Mr. . . . .?"

"Do not alarm yourself, Malcolm MacGow. We knew your father, and we know you from a distance," said the figure. "It is now time that we meet face to face as the hour grows near that death seeks to claim you as its own." As the figure stepped forward, a stream of light shone across his face, illuminating only his eyes to Malcolm, who stood with anticipation for the identity of this individual. His hands moved to his hood as he threw it back over his head and allowed it to fall down onto his back. "I am Sean Macgalloglass, son of Adam, originally from Ireland."

"Druids . . ." Malcolm spoke. "I wondered if I would ever get to meet any of you. I'm so sorry for the death of one of your members. I saw his body yesterday at the Tolbooth."

"We were unable to protect him because his special mission required him to act alone. I can tell you though that he killed several of the Enlightened Ones, which is what they call themselves."

"What kind of organization are they and what do they want?"

"They are a splinter group of individuals that make up a larger group which originated in Rome more years ago than I know. They will masquerade as whatever they need to be to accomplish their goals. This group took control of Forfar back in 1661 and used witch trials to further their goals. This same thing happened all over Europe and was actually worse in other countries. I don't believe that all of these churches were so bad that they thought the same way and condemned all those innocent people to death. The Enlightened Ones took advantage of their fears and used the Bible to make the claims that they presented to the Elders to justify their means," Sean said.

"Sean, do you know Theodore Higginbottom?" Malcolm asked. "Yes, I do. I had firsthand dealings with him years ago. Your father saved me from him and his men."

"I have heard that he is in the colonies, perpetrating the same scheme over there. My brother is there at this time, and I am greatly concerned about him. Also, someone killed my friend up in Killiemuir, and I assume it was this organization you speak of," Malcolm said. "Yes, the very same, I'm afraid. They have never fully gone away and seek to find a way to revive their fear—mongering ways once again. I'm also sure they poisoned your father years ago. They never forget old scores to settle," spoke Sean. "It is for this purpose that we were sent from Ireland to combat these horrible men. The Druids here in Scotland are just not equipped to handle such a well organized group as these Enlightened Ones. You see, Malcolm, we are more than just Druids: we are heavily armed Druid soldiers specially trained to handle the more sophisticated elements of society. We once ruled large sections of Europe and controlled many Celtic societies. We were intermediaries between the Celtic people and their gods. Our main downfall was the Romans. We were persecuted by them to the point of extinction and barely survive today. It is from the Romans that Higginbottom's organization sprang, and they are still fulfilling their mission today. The Romans were never able to conquer Scotland and had to build walls to protect themselves from the Picts who were the dominant fighters."

"So the Druids and the Enlightened Ones have coexisted in a sort of never-ending battle for all these years?" Malcolm asked.

"Yes, we have. We had no choice. If we fail, we feel that an evil cloud will overtake mankind, and we will all fall under the control of people who will enslave and use us for their master's world domination."

"Well, I have a son to protect and a brother to look after, and I for one am not going down to this group or any other. If my father thought it this important to support your mission, then we will too. I'd like to know more about your history and that of the Enlightened Ones if I could," Malcolm replied.

"I will tell you what you need to know so that you will have a better understanding of why we have to act against this group. Your father was very active with us and believed our message, but was more comfortable with his Christian religion, which we respect immensely. Many of us are Christian and were converted many years ago. Druids are more similar to Christians than people know. We do not sacrifice people on an altar and never have. Our enemies have conjured up many lies to sway the public against us. We have played a very important part in society through the years in keeping peace and harmony in everyday life. We were advisers to kings and performed the functions of teachers, healers, and judges."

"Please, Sean, have a seat on the hay bale and make yourself comfortable," Malcolm proposed.

As the Druid sat cross-legged on the bale, Malcolm heard strange rattlings from the Druid's robes. Noticing that Malcolm heard the noise, Sean assured Malcolm that he had to protect himself and thatwhat he heard was just his defensive hardware.

"We war against a well equipped enemy, and we must stay as far ahead of them as we can. I know it probably confuses you concerning our image, but we have always had our own hierarchy of Druids withvarious duties. Some of us are protectors," Sean said.

"What part did my father play in your hierarchy? Did he achieve a rank of any kind?" Malcolm asked.

"He was never a fully ordained Druid, but he did gain ample knowledge of how things worked. You will be proud to know that he was accepted to be baptized in one of the most sacred sites in our part of the world. Robert was allowed to go and was escorted to Dartmoor, England, to the Druid's Stone."

"The Druid's Stone? I've never heard my father speak of it. Why is it so special?" Malcolm asked.

"Those who were handpicked and deemed to be of 'universal potential' were sent to the Druid's Stone. It was a large stone with a hole carved through it many eons ago that will accommodate a man who can slip through it into the river below. Streams of light at a certain time of day and certain time of the year allow the baptized person to be immersed in a bath of light right before he slips through the hole into the water. This was indeed a very special place to be sent. Not many went there," Sean said.

"My father preferred Christianity then over Druidism but still respected your ways and helped you when necessary."

"That is the choice he made, and we all accepted it. The Druid order always held your father in high esteem."

"The magistrate assured me that he would provide whatever men he could spare to protect Ian and me from any attacks. I don't really think that he can be everywhere at once. What do you suggest?" Malcolm asked.

"We will protect you to the best of our abilities and make sure no harm comes to you and your house. We will be here, even if you can't see us. It's one of those things that we do well. Just go about your daily tasks as you normally would and show no fear to this enemy," the Druid spoke.

Malcolm understood what the Druid expected of him, but showing no fear and acting normal in the face of what had recently taken place was going to be harder than it looked. However, Malcolm was determined to do what the Druid suggested. He noticed that the Druid was very calm and gave the appearance of someone who was not excitable and would act slowly in response to an attack. He knew though that this was not the case, for the stories had been related to him by his father about how Druids were surprisingly decisive in taking out an enemy. They were swift killers when they had to be, and after hearing all the hardware sounds from beneath the Druid's robe, he didn't want to be on the receiving end of whatever he carried. "Sean, explain to me why it was the Romans that the Druids were basically at war with from early times," Malcolm wanted to know. "You see, Rome once ruled the world and eventually conquered all the way to the British Isles. In between Rome and the isles were the Druids. We were in most of the countries that the Romans came into to subjugate. Our ways presented a threat to them because our science and philosophy contradicted Roman orthodoxy. Romans were materialistic while

Druids were spiritual. Romans looked upon women as bearers of children and objects of pleasure; Druids would include women in their religious and political processes. The Roman Empire is gone, but Druid splinter groups that were never extinguished still stay loyal to their original purpose. Druids have dwindled to the point of near extinction, but we still fight on for our way of life and our commitments," Sean continued. "We have to operate in a most secret way these days due to the rise of Christianity and its intolerance. We do continue to practice the things we have been taught though and strive to pass our teachings on to our families and friends. All of our teachings are oral. This has always been our way," Sean said. "Malcolm, I must tell you that your brother will encounter trouble in the colonies, but he is being guarded by my father, Adam, and two other Druids who traveled to the colonies with Daniel. Your brother is not aware of his guardians though," Sean said.

"I will leave you now and implement the plan to protect you and Ian. We have more Druids in this area than you might suspect. Be of good faith, Malcolm."

As Malcolm began to pace back and forth near the cooling forge, he began to talk either to himself or the Druid, trying to work off the energy that had built up with the tension and conversation with the Druid. "I want the killers of my friend Alasdair and your Druid brother brought to justice if nothing else is accomplished. I want to see the . . . Enlightened . . . Ones." Malcolm now noticed that the Druid was gone, without a sound or good-bye. The same door that had creaked when he came through it had not made a sound on his departure.

The next day, Malcolm was to meet with Kate once more, and he was anxious to see her. Kate and Malcolm had decided to meet in the same place they had met earlier— down the dead-end road. What Kate didn't know was that Malcolm had remembered her birthday from one of their past conversations and had brought her a present. He knew she would be pleased with the gift. When Malcolm arrived, he only had to wait a few minutes before Kate arrived also. She was very punctual and hated to be kept waiting by someone, even Malcolm. He had learned this the hard way already. Pulling her carriage alongside of Malcolm's, she was helped up into his and they sat for awhile. They greeted each other with a kiss that actually made Kate, "aah" when the kiss was broken. Malcolm always knew that his kiss was special when she made that sound. He enjoyed her so much that he had a hard time putting into words the way he felt for her. He tried to tell her but would stumble over his thoughts and never quite get the true meaning out. He would tell her he loved her, which was very easy to understand, but he just wanted to give her a stronger message of how he felt.

"Kate, you look beautiful today. You're so pretty and smell so good today," Malcolm said.

"I've missed you so much and couldn't wait to see you— and on such a hot day,"Kate said.

"It sure is. I have something for you that might take your mind off the heat." Reaching into his bag, Malcolm pulled out a framed picture of angels flying in the night sky. "You made the comment that you liked this awhile back, and so I got it for you. Happy Birthday, Kate," Malcolm said.

"I do like it. Thank you very much." She kissed Malcolm again. "I know you told me your age, but, Kate, you don't look it at all. You are truly beautiful, and I love you!" Malcolm said in a soft and tender way.

"Malcolm, you make me feel like I have a future; if only I could have met you years ago when I was unattached. Where were you?" Kate said in an inquisitive manner.

"Fate just didn't want us to meet then, I suppose. The main thing is we're together now and we can be with each other forever if you want to. It's up to us, Kate," Malcolm said.

"Are you sure you want to give up everything for me that you've built up over the years?" Kate said.

"You fill every void in my life, Kate. Of course I do. You are my princess, the girl I've been waiting for all these years. I would do anything for you, Kate, anything."

"You are so special to me. I'm not used to having someone say to me, 'I love you,' like you do all the time. I'm not used to the compliments and the special attention you give. Do you really feel this way, Malcolm?"

"Aye! I say these things from the heart, not to blindly pass out compliments for your amusement. I mean every one of them. I love you with all that's within me, Kate. Please believe me," Malcolmexclaimed.

After several hours of talking, holding hands, and enjoying each other's kisses, Kate and Malcolm said their good-byes and went on with their daily routines. Even apart, they were not really separated. They thought about each other constantly, reliving all that they had said and done while together and thinking about where they could go and what they would do the next time out.

Malcolm went back to his forge and started back on the orders he had to do for his customers. It was time to, once more, get dirty with soot and sweat as he pounded the iron into the shapes the customers expected. Ian was hauling in supplies to make sure they had all the materials necessary to keep the orders flowing. He would stack the metal into sections so they could count their inventory and also be able to grab exactly what they needed to work on. Lots of swords and knives were usually the order of the day, but horseshoing was also a constant with Malcolm. It was good that Malcolm had Ian there because of the riding lessons that Malcolm gave as a sideline business. The way Malcolm saw it, he was preparing another generation that would eventually need his services. Keep them interested in horses, and they would need shoeing at some time. Malcolm would also add metal to the shields that the clansmen would use in battle to add strength to the wood and keep it fastened together in battle.

"Malcolm, how's my sword coming along? You never know when a Campbell might be lurking around to stir up trouble," said one of Malcolm's steady customers.

"Your sword is already finished, Christopher. Ian, did you not deliver Mr. Gracie's sword to him yet, lad?"

"Aye, that I did, but he was not at home, so I brought it back here. I didn't want to leave it and have it stolen, not a fine weapon like that," Ian said. "I'll get it right away, Mr. Gracie."

"A very responsible boy you have there, Malcolm. He's going to be a good one indeed."

"He's already a good one. I trust him thoroughly," Malcolm said.

"Here you are, sir. I hope it meets your expectations," Ian said.

"Ah, it's a splendid piece of craftsmanship. You MacGows never disappoint." Christopher Gracie took a few swings in the air, looked down the length of it as he closed one eye to get a fix on the smooth line from handle to tip, and smiled. "Thanks again. I'll be the envy of the clan with this fine piece. Good day to you both."

Ian walked Mr. Gracie out of the forge and mingled with some other local men who had gathered to talk about the weather, the political scene, or just some other person who happened to not be present. People were going to and fro on the busy road, everyone with their own business to attend. As Malcolm began the process of closing down the forge for the evening, he noticed a man on horseback whom he couldn't place. He was pretty sure that the man was not a local as the man pulled the reins of his horse back and forth, for the horse had become a bit skittish. He suddenly pointed the horse in the direction of the group of people that Ian was a part of and started a steady jog toward them. Malcolm became concerned that the man might be looking at Ian and might be someone from the group that the Druid had talked about earlier. Malcolm, ripping off his thick gloves one at a time, threw them down on the forge floor and started a fast paced walk toward the same location where Ian was. Realizing that his gait wouldn't get him to Ian before the man on horseback, Malcolm started to run toward the group. As the man on horseback arrived, just seconds before Malcolm, Malcolm heard him say, "Thomas MacBain, I thought that was you." The man on the horse brought his steed to a fast halt in front of the group.

"George MacInnes! I thought you a dead man," said Mr. MacBain.

"In the flesh, alive and kicking, never felt better." He gave a hearty laugh. Dismounting and trying to calm the horse, he shook the hand of his longtime friend, Mr. MacBain.

Malcolm had brought his own run to a stop just shy of Ian as Ian turned around to his dad. "Dad, everything alright?"

"Yes, I thought . . . for a moment I . . . oh nothing, Ian." Malcolm felt relief but also embarrassment for thinking what he didn't tell Ian. But how was he to know if the man was aiming for Ian? After all, he was a stranger, and Ian was so vulnerable. Malcolm walked back into the forge, took the dipper from the bucket, and poured water over his head before taking a long cool drink. Malcolm's heart was racing at a pretty good pace as the adrenaline pumped through his body. He had been ready to fight to defend his son, and now it was over, that quickly. Malcolm knew though that he could never let his guard down with what was lurking in the shadows of this village. He had to see this thing through to the end, just in order to survive, for there would never be rest for him and Ian as long as the threat existed and they were the targets.

Eleven

A s Daniel awoke from a rather restful sleep, he remarked to himself how peaceful and alert he was. He could not remember ever having had such a calm, easy sleep before. He was not groggy or in a morning stupor, but was energized and ready to take on the day. He thought about what he had to face outside the cave in the form of Mr. Higginbottom and wondered what he had to do to stay ahead of this adversary. Apparently, one of the Druids had already awakened and lit a few candles to provide a light since they were in a cave. There was a small opening in the roof of the cave, which allowed the smoke to filter through so the cave remained clear and breathable. Daniel looked around the room and noticed that he was the last to wake up. The other Druids were up or not in the cave. Breakfast was ready to be served, but it was an uncooked one. They lit no fires this morning, fearing the smoke would draw attention to them— all because the Druids knew that Mr. Higginbottom would not rest until he recaptured Daniel. Daniel was one prisoner that he would not allow to escape forever. Mr. Higginbottom had special plans for him. This was a family feud that was not going to be settled peacefully.

"That was a very tasty meal you served last night, Adam. You'll have to give me the recipe."

"Oh, and do you appreciate the fine art of dining and food preparation?" Adam asked Daniel.

"Yes, sir, I do. If you could ask my brother, he'd tell you just how much. I'm the . . . or was, the family chef before coming to the colonies. I taught my nephew all I could before my departure so my brother wouldn't starve to death," Daniel said in a lighthearted way.

"Then you must know about the herb, agrimony. Richard put in a pinch last night as you may already have noticed because of the way you slept. Do you feel any different than you normally do when you awoke this morning?" Adam asked.

"Aye, most certainly. I am not familiar with that herb. Where does it derive from, if I may ask?" Daniel asked.

"Why, from Scotland of course. Surely you must have come across it in your studies of the various edible herbs of the countryside," Adam said.

"That one seems to have escaped me, Adam," Daniel said. "I thought I knew most of the tasty ones at least. Where in Scotland does that one originate?"

"In a place called Loch Ewe where it is reputed to be from a magic garden,"Adam said.

"Well, if I ever get back to Scotland, I'll certainly have that excursion to look forward to," Daniel said.

As Daniel and Adam finished their conversation, Charles came into the room from the tunnel entrance. "There's no sign of movement in the surrounding forest, and none of our traps have been disturbed," Charles said.

"That is excellent! We have work to do, and not having nosey neighbors around will help us immensely. Daniel, what plans do you have for your future?"Adam asked.

"Since I have been on the run, I have not had time to think it through. I can't go to my cabin for my supplies, and I don't know a whole lot of people I want to trust right now."

"We will tell you this much; we are here for you only. Our duty is to keep you safe, that your life may continue. We live to serve and give back to those who deserve our trust. Your family is deserving of that trust. Our Druid code is best served this way. Although there be fewer of us in the world, we still honor our ancestors and our pledges," Adam said.

"I count you all as friends. I appreciate you being there for me and protecting me. I was always self-sufficient and able to take care of myself, able to fight my own fights and figure things out for myself, but now it seems I've come up against a foe that has me outnumbered and outfoxed with the local government on his side. I can't fight them all, Adam, and I'm distressed. I've never felt this helpless before— never like this," Daniel lamented.

"What do you want to do, Daniel? How do you want to handle your situation? We will comply with whatever you want," Adam said. "I want to stop the activities of Higginbottom and help the poor people who are suffering in Salem Village. The madness there is reprehensible and those responsible should be brought to justice."

"Sometimes, the best way is to step back and gather your thoughts and composure. You may well be better equipped for the fight after that. I'm not saying you should abandon your quest, but rather take another avenue. You might want to retreat until they think you are gone for good, dead or lost to them. They will eventually give up hope of finding you, and then you could return to fight another day. You would be able to plan your strategy and take them on your terms. You could cleanse your soul and be at peace with yourself and have your goals made clear," Adam said.

"The only place for me to have peace and security is with the Indians west of here. I have been where no white man has gone. I have been the only Scot they have ever seen. We understand each other and can commune with each other and the earth. Higginbottom and his men would never be able to track me there. But I don't want to feel like I'm deserting those that need help," Daniel said.

"We will honor whatever decision you make. However, we will not venture into the Indian territories. This is something you will have to do on your own. We will wait here in this area for your return as we turn our attention to Mr. Higginbottom. If things change here and we see that it is safe for you to return, we will get word to you," Adam said.

"Then it is settled. I will venture into Iroquois land and live among them. I know I will be safe, and I can hunt to pay my keep. I have become good friends with their chief, and it would be good to see him once again."

"We will give you all the supplies you need to make your journey and will walk with you part of the way. We wish for you to be safe and secure in your being and to gather your thoughts for future service to this colony. I have a feeling that you will play a very important part in it," Adam said.

As Daniel gathered his supplies, he felt thankful for these Druids who had rescued him. He now felt that he was not just being pushed around or swayed from here to there. Even back in Scotland with the stories of his father, to whom he now wished he had paid more attention, he realized that his family was watched over or influenced by Druids. He hadn't cared at the time; he went about living his own life, being self-indulgent while trying to make his mark. He didn't want to stay in the blacksmith field, for to him that was not enough challenge and was mundane at best. He could have been a great chef, for he loved to cook up so many different recipes that delighted the palate. But again, he needed more to keep him going forward in life. He just had not been ready to settle down to a normal career and surrender his motivation to life itself. He thought about the time when he had hit upon the idea of travel— not just to another county or local country, but to another part of the world. He had thought about the navy— joining the British fleet and seeing what was on the other side of the world. He wanted the adventure of meeting people of foreign habitation and learning how they lived, being part of a great sailing vessel of a world power as she made her way to ports not her own. Yes, he had thought about this idea, but he knew that after a while, he would feel confined on a ship that at first might appear enormous, but after months at sea would feel like a woodshed. He wouldn't be able to stand that. No, he had wanted something else and then it had hit him: the Colonies— a new area where he wouldn't be held back or confined to a small geographical area. He could walk or ride as far as he wanted to travel. He could make his way without interference and never reach the end of his desire to move forward. The Colonies, where he could use his abilities to explore the limits of his own imagination, and make his fortune if he applied himself and was not a lazy and drunken sot. It was such a place that Daniel ventured to— a place where no one knew him and he could make friends anew and fit in or not fit in. He could be his own man and direct his own future. He could come and go as he pleased. Realizing that he was now a man on the run didn't change how he felt about his own philosophy concerning his life. This was apparently a part of his destiny, and the Druids helped him to see this. Life was an adventure in itself.

As they pushed forward through the forest heading west, they had traveled only about two miles when Adam knew that something was amiss. People could be seen on both sides of them carrying arms. With swords and pistols tucked into heavy belts, the men looked their way with tired, haggard looks on their faces. Men were now ahead of them and behind them as they scanned the area, looking for the avenue of least resistance.

"Seems like we have company, Adam," Daniel said. "I haven't had enough exercise for the last twenty-four hours, so it's time to flex a little muscle. I hope you're armed beneath those robes, Adam." Even as Daniel spoke, Richard and Charles were already drawing Scottish made swords that were quite impressive.

"My brother could have made that piece a lot fancier if you had have given him the order," Daniel remarked.

"Your brother did make this weapon years ago, but didn't know who we were at the time, which was our desire," Adam said.

Daniel also drew his sword that had been given to him by Charles back at the cave. Seeing that the circle of followers closed in tighter, Daniel knew that not much talking was going to take place. The foes that they faced had determination etched into their eyes as if they had been sorely wronged by those they pursued. As Adam weighed their options, he decided that they needed to have the best position available, and that seemed to be up against a high rock formation, so at least they would be able to see their adversaries advance on them. "Daniel, head for the rocks to your left and find the best point to turn to make your defense. Take the higher ground and hold it."

As they started their run to the rocks, their adversaries gave chase, converging on the four figures. As some of the pursuers were faster than the rest, two of them caught up to Daniel's group much quicker. "Richard, behind you, now!" Adam yelled out. As quick as any cat Daniel had ever seen, Richard swung around and, with a single stroke, cut down the nearest attacker before the man knew what had happened. The other man halted just for a second out of complete and utter surprise at the audacity of his foe, and that was all the time Richard needed to remove his head from his body. As the blood splattered on Richard's tunic and the surrounding trees, he retraced his steps to the area Adam had designated as their stronghold. Arriving just behind the other three, Richard took up his position and awaited the wave of attackers to come at them. He didn't have long to wait as the killing of their brothers egged them on even more. There had to be at least fifteen or more of them as they ran headlong into the area where Daniel and the Druids were waiting. As the first wave of attackers arrived, swords on both sides were swinging and hacking at whatever was before them. Several attackers were cut down, but Charles had been set upon by three of them at once and fell as too many blades found their marks through his body. Daniel received a gash on his forearm before he cut down the man who had engaged him first. Adam suggested that they climb as high as they could over the boulders and maybe find a way of escape near the top. The going was difficult, for the rocks were moist from the morning dew. Several of the attackers were trying to flank them and cut off their escape route. As they tediously made their way, two of the enemy caught up with Richard, tripping him up and taking him as prisoner. He was quickly bound and made to lie on the rocks just below Daniel and Adam. "You can stop running; we have your friend. We promise no one will be further hurt if you surrender Daniel MacGow to us immediately," spoke one of the pursuers with a large black moustache. Daniel and Adam halted their climb and turned to see that, indeed, Richard had been made their prisoner and was totally helpless in their hands. "Keep going," Richard bellowed at the top of his lungs. "Don't worry about me."

"Well, what will it be? You and your friend here can go on your way; just give us Daniel."

"I can't ask you to risk any more for me. I'm turning myself in," Daniel said to Adam.

"You don't know the Druid way, Daniel. We are not afraid of death and, at times, welcome it. Richard has no fear of these men. We should do as he requests and continue our escape."

"I just can't risk any more of you getting killed for me; I'm going down to them. It will be an even exchange— my life for his— then you both can be on your way."

As Daniel started his climb back down the rocks, there was a sudden scuffle down below with Richard and the attackers. Richard had used his legs to trip one of his guards, knocking him off the rocks to fall to the jagged edges below. Regaining his footing and standing up, he rammed his body into another guard as they both tumbled off the cliff to certain death below. Daniel couldn't believe what had just taken place. It had happened so quickly that he couldn't quite comprehend this action on Richard's part. The rest of the attackers were just as shocked as anyone and turned their attention back up the rock face to Daniel and Adam.

"Now you can believe, Daniel. Now you know a little bit more about us. Richard provided you another chance. Let's not disappoint him. We have to go. Now!"

Daniel looked for just another second or two before reality set in and he knew that running was the only option left. "To hell with you all! Come and get me," Daniel challenged his pursuers. Turning around quickly, he took giant steps as he climbed back to where Adam was.

"Okay, let's put some distance between us and them," Adam said. "Let's make a stand and fight. There's not nearly as many of them left and I know we could take them," Daniel said to Adam.

"We will flee, Daniel. You have to know when to fight and when to make a hasty retreat. I'm sure you know this country better than they do as you are one of only a few white men who have even ventured out west. Use your knowledge of the wilderness and lose them there. They will eventually have to break off pursuit as they become unfamiliar to the area and the hostile natives there. You, on the other hand, will be welcomed."

"You are right. Let's go."

Traveling as fast as they could traverse the wilderness, Daniel and Adam made very good time and outran their pursuers. They paused by a stream to drink away their thirst and cool their heads, catching their breath and gathering their thoughts. The last hour or so seemed like a dream to Daniel; the fight and the deaths of his adversaries, not counting his Druid friend Richard who had sacrificed his life for him, seemed unreal. Yes, he did know now what the Druids were about. They had their own code of conduct, which not only included dedication to service, but even the act of laying one's life down for a friend. He had even learned a little more about his own father and his connection to the Druids simply by living with them the past few days. They were truly remarkable people.

Daniel looked at Adam and saw that he was always alert. His eyes looked to and fro for any enemy or danger that would threaten them. He was forever diligent. Daniel also made note of the fact that when Adam drank from the stream, he kept his head fixed on the horizon and his eyes moving as he dipped his hand into the water and brought the water to his mouth. He would not look directly into the stream. Adam had cuts and a few nasty gashes on his arms and legs. He kept pressure on them but did not treat them.

"Adam, let me tend to your wounds if I could. You've got a few scraps there that need fixing." Daniel had torn a few pieces of material from his sack and wrapped Adam's wounds the best he could under the circumstances. He knew Adam was appreciative for this act as he nodded his okay.

"I will gather herbs to dress these later when I'm sure we're safe. I suggest we keep moving for the time being," Adam said.

As they gathered their things, Daniel noticed the sky was turning grayer and a few raindrops had started to fall. As the wind picked up, leaves whirled up all around them while windblown branches swayed back and forth, creaking out an almost rhythmic sound to their ears as if someone were pushing and pulling the branches on a timed scale. Adam pulled the hood cloak tighter around his head, and Daniel buttoned his coat and pulled up the collar around his neck. The noise of the wind made it difficult for them to hear each other, so they had to raise their voices to communicate. As Adam was explaining their next move to Daniel, lightning crashed not far from them causing Daniel to jump from the sudden explosion of sound. Adam took it in stride as though he hadn't heard a thing.

"We need to find shelter until this blows over," Adam said. AsDaniel strained his eyes through the heavy downpour and wind, hecould see a stand of heavy pine trees that had ample branches providing a natural canopy and at least some protection from the wind and possibly the rain as well. Daniel and Adam made a beeline to the spot, ducking under the long swaying branches, some of which touched the ground. This was going to be the best they could find for the present time. It was remarkably dry underneath considering how hard the rain was coming down. They still feared the lightning though, and Daniel jumped a little on each thundering bolt that struck near them. Only a few drops here and there would soak through their new home for the present. They tried to dry off and make the best of the situation for now. They found some dry branches and twigs which Adam used to start a fire. Daniel started to prepare more strips of cloth to bandage their wounds now that they had time to rest.

"I know you didn't want to be with me at this stage of the journey, and I want you to know that I appreciate your company. If things had gone the way we planned, I would be halfway to where I should be and you would be . . . Where would you be, Adam?"

"I would be making my way to Salem Village to finish my mission of derailing Mr. Higginbottom. Of course, now my job will beconsiderably harder without my two companions to assist me, but it's still not impossible. I will just have to improvise. On the other hand, I'm still protecting you, which is my main concern in this whole affair."

"Tell me, Adam. Why is it that you won't or can't continue with me into Indian territory? Are you afraid?"

"You really have to ask that? You think I fear the Indians?""No, not really. I spoke too soon. I've seen your courage, and I actually know better. Then what is it, Adam?"

"Even in Scotland, we have heard of the power the Indians have with their magic and spiritual prowess and believe that what we have and what they possess would collide, cancelling out both of our means of achieving protection and harmony with nature. You see, Daniel, we are very possessive with what we have learned and what has been passed down through the centuries from each generation and . . . well. . . we are jealous of our powers and abilities. We're just from two different worlds that must not be mingled and mixed. It's best for them and us to keep apart. This might be hard for you to understand, you not being a Druid, but it does make sense to us. Long ago, some three hundred years ago, Druids sailed to the New World with the Sinclairs. As far as they knew, they were the first to set foot on this colonial land, at least where they laid anchor. There may have been Vikings before, but not as far south as we went. According to Druid brothers, they encountered local tribes and had conflicts from the very beginning. We respect their ways, but we must stay separate. As Adam and Daniel prepared to bed down for the night, Daniel made the fire ready and supplied enough extra wood to keep them warm and dry until the morning. The rations they had were for quick meals— nothing fancy, but enough to survive on. Daniel knew he would have to hunt small game along the way anyway. Druids were just as adept at catching an evening meal as any hunter on the continent, and Adam might have to prove it if things stayed the same. "I could sure go for some venison stew right now," Daniel said to Adam, rubbing his stomach in circular motions.

"I could too, but it's about too late for hunting today; better make do with our pack rations for the night," Adam remarked.

As they prepared and ate their evening meal, they had just about dried their clothing and were getting ready to turn in for the night. The storm was still brewing, and on occasion the lightning would light up the whole camp area. All they could do was hope the storm would run its course and be finished by the morning so they could get their bearings to plot their course for the day.

"Daniel, you know that I will be leaving you tomorrow to return back to civilization again. You are safe from Higginbottom's men and are well able to fend for yourself from this point on. Agreed?" Adam said.

"Aye, but I'm going to miss your company, my friend. Will you still be back there when I return?"

"I will wait for you forever. My mission has not changed and I will be faithful to my calling."

"Hopefully, Higginbottom will be a nasty memory when I do return— he and that whole bunch of scoundrels."

Nightfall had settled in and the woods became as black as a cave.Only the firepit and occasional lightning bolts striking through the night sky gave illumination to their world now. Daniel had thrown on some additional logs for the fire to help keep them warm through the night as they slowly dozed off into a well deserved dream world. As the morning slowly awoke the forest, the creatures that lived there were calling the new day into being with all their animal sounds and commotions. Birds were annoyingly loud as they seemed to be drawing the whole earth to attention just because they liked to get up early. Daniel and Adam had slept through the night, undisturbed and dead to the world. Their bodies needed the rest from the previous day's activities, which were not a common agenda of events. The two men under the pine tree stretched and moaned as they found it hard to believe that it could be morning already. The fire was no longer burning, but a steady plume of smoke wafted from its embers and rose through the tree boughs and branches, heading to wherever the wind would take it. It was after Adam and Daniel cleared their eyes and minds of the dream world they had just come from that it hit them at the same time . . . they had company! Standing all around the camp were what looked like most of the Iroquois nation, men painted in the most odd fashion with designs that made no real sense to Daniel and especially not to Adam. They, for the most part, had spears and bow and arrows pointed toward the camp, without making any noise and standing almost motionless. They made no facial movements as well. They waited and watched. Waiting for what? For Daniel and Adam to say something or make a false move? The two men suddenly became frozen with the same look as their Indian counterparts. They didn't want to risk any movement that might cause one of them to loose an arrow or throw a spear toward them.

"It would appear, Adam, that we have come much farther than I thought. I've never seen Indian people this far toward the villages before," Daniel said to Adam.

"I am Daniel. Daniel MacGow. I have hunted in your land before. I am friends with your chief. May I see him, please?" Daniel said hopefully.

"Your kind we have seen before. What is his kind?" said one of the Indians, pointing toward Adam.

"He is a Druid. He is from a far off land across the mighty waters.He is like you in that he worships the Great Spirit in the Sky. He is my friend. We come in peace and wish your people no harm." As Daniel studied the situation, he assessed that this was a large hunting party. What they were doing this far from their own hunting grounds was beyond Daniel's understanding. As some of the Iroquois were examining Adam and his strange cloak, the men of the hunting party suddenly started to part and stand to one side. As the last of the group stepped back, they revealed three white men whom Daniel identified by their clothing as French. "Now what would the French be doing on this side of the boundary that separates British territory from French?" Daniel thought to himself.

"Monsieur, what, may I ask, are you and your friend doing out here alone in the wilderness?" one of the Frenchmen asked.

"We thought we might ask you the same question, mon ami," Daniel said.

"You don't seem to be in any position to ask anything, Monsieur. Now, I ask you one more time, what is your business here?"

As the Frenchman ended his question, several of the Iroquois jumped to attention and pointed their spears at Daniel and Adam as if it was a final opportunity to comply. Daniel thought it time to speak up and tell them why they were here.

"We were escaping our attackers, many miles back east of here. Two of our party were killed, and so we had to flee," Daniel said. " I was coming to my friends, the Iroquois, for sanctuary and a place to live until times were more settled in Salem. My companion here was escorting me to a safe place and was planning on returning to Salem this very day," Daniel pleaded. "You have my word on this as my friends in the Iroquois Nation can substantiate."

"I believe you . . . uh, Monsieur. It is of utmost regret though that I must insist you both come with me back to the Nation, only temporarily you see, for everyone's safety, oui?"

"Aye, we will comply." Daniel knew something was obviously not right, but did not have enough information to assess the situation. What were they planning, being this far from home, and how did the Iroquois fit into it all? Daniel knew that the Iroquois were friendly with the French, but were they plotting something sinister? Lots of questions but no answers. Daniel and Adam resigned themselves to the fact that they were basically prisoners, but at least they weren't bound ones. They would have to wait and see. Daniel hoped he wasn't getting himself into a worse situation.

Twelve

"So, Dad, what are we to do with this organization the Druids told us about?" Ian asked. "We're just average hardworking men who are trying to make a living and not looking to hurt anyone. How did we end up being the focus of their attention? Why us?"

"You're right. We are average hardworking men, but apparently we are a little more than that, at least to this sinister group. We're going to have to participate in their game whether we want to or not, even if it's just to survive them," Malcolm said.

As the days went along, Malcolm had no contact with any unusual characters nor any out of the ordinary circumstances. He had worked most days in the forge from early morning to sundown, and everything was calm and normal, as if nothing was amiss. But Malcolm harbored a sense of anticipation of dread that hung over him and his house. He knew the threat had not just evaporated but was like a clever hunter, waiting for the chance to strike. Malcolm was forever diligent in maintaining his guard even if he looked at ease. He conducted his life as always, but with great hidden caution.

As Malcolm and Ian were conducting their business in the forge, Malcolm remembered a meeting he had to attend at the church tomorrow. Several men from town wanted to share some information that they thought would be of benefit to Malcolm and also to show their concern and support for him and Ian.

"Ian, I'm calling it a day. Can you close down for the night when you're finished, son? Tomorrow I'll be attending a meeting with some townsfolk.If you'll open in the morning, I'll catch up to you later by noon."

"Aye, I'll do it!" Ian actually loved the procedure of opening and closing the forge. It gave him a sense of control and importance as though he needed to feel that way. Malcolm knew just how important Ian was to the success of the business and was appreciative. What Malcolm didn't tell Ian was that he was first going to visit with Kate and spend some time with her before the meeting. Ian didn't need to know everything Malcolm was doing. He didn't want to address any questions that Ian might ask, so to avoid that situation, he kept some things to himself.

The morning came, and Malcolm was up making a small breakfast that was quick and easy. He didn't want to disturb Ian since he had been late to bed last night and was opening the forge this morning. He washed up and made himself presentable since he was meeting the girl he loved. He was out the door and into the barn to hitch his horse to his carriage and then off for a ride to the meeting place they had prearranged. Malcolm arrived first at the rendezvous point and waited patiently for Kate. The place they were meeting was by a stream that came out of the mountains with very cold water, a most beautiful and picturesque location. It was only minutes until Kate arrived and pulled her carriage up next to Malcolm's. Malcolm jumped down from his carriage as Kate came down and walked around to meet him. As she walked toward Malcolm, he thought at that point, she looked the best he had ever seen her. To him, she was the most spectacular creature on God's green earth. As she got within arm's reach, they took each other in their arms for a close hug and then a soft kiss that they refused to break.

"I've missed you so much, Malcolm. I couldn't wait to see you again," Kate said.

"And I've missed you the same, Kate. I love you! You look really nice today. I've not seen you in this outfit before, but it definitely suits you just fine."

Malcolm looked deep within her eyes as he stared, mesmerized by her beauty. Her blue eyes were pools of liquid pleasure to Malcolm with her soft white complexion and blond hair. To Malcolm, she was truly a classy lady. To him, she had no flaws.Although she herself often complained and was constantly pointing her flaws out to Malcolm, he didn't see it that way. He was perfectly happy with her just the way she was. On this particular day, Kate had brought along a family portrait to show Malcolm. It showed her and her parents when she was younger. Kate had confided that both of her parents were now deceased. Malcolm didn't at first believe that it was even her, but the more he looked, the more she came into focus. Her face had been fuller when she was younger, but Malcolm thought she was getting prettier with age. The fact that she showed Malcolm this family portrait also showed him that she trusted him at a different level than she would someone else. She was very open about her family and didn't mind discussing personal happenings. She confided in him and knew he would keep her confidences and secrets. She was falling in love with him and bringing him closer to her with each meeting. Although she was constantly looking over her shoulder just in case someone would see her with Malcolm, knowing she was betrothed to someone else, she still would not stop seeing Malcolm and desiring to be with him every chance she got. She could only reason that she had not experienced life the way she should have through the years with being too concerned about what others thought about her— about how her parents had made up her mind for her too often. Even this engagement to her present fiancé wasn't totally her idea, but it was socially acceptable. It seemed that love was secondary to the relationship. But there was something about Malcolm that was so very different from past relationships. It wasn't something that she could even put into words if one were to analyze Malcolm and her coming together. She just knew it was different and right.

Malcolm could not get enough of her and wanted very badly to be with her every day, but he knew that was not possible with their separate lives and responsibilities. She would often rearrange her weekly schedule to accommodate Malcolm so they could be together. Even this act made Malcolm feel like he was very important to her. He deeply appreciated that gesture. One of the little things that she would do to Malcolm was compliment him on the shape of his ears. He never considered such an appendage to be that important, at least not on him, but she did. She would kiss his earlobes, which would give Malcolm goose bumps on his arms and neck. He never complained. Everything she wanted to do, Malcolm was in favor of. She made him feel like the man he hadn't been in a long time. He enjoyed the attention and the compliments. He wished that he could have her go home with him permanently, that they might never be apart again. This was the frustrating part of the relationship— the parting of ways until the next meeting.

"Kate, I want you to know that since I met you I have had no urge to be with anyone else, no desire to court or even to look at anyone else. You have changed me into a person I never thought I would ever be. To be perfectly honest with you, I never would have believed it possible of me. My passion and desire are for you alone. You are my queen, and I love you more than life itself."

"Malcolm, to be totally honest with you too, I've never used the 'I love you' phrase more than I have with you. I too never thought it possible."

As their time came to an end for this rendezvous, the hardest part was saying their good-byes. They kissed each other in the most passionate way possible and enjoyed the exchange of their love with each other. Kate would often tell Malcolm that when they kissed each other very deeply, they were exchanging and intermingling their very souls with one another. Malcolm had never heard that before, but felt as if it were a truth he had always known. This was a truth revealed to him, and he fully embraced it. It was a feeling deeper than any act two people could ever commit. Where had she been for so long, where had he been for so long, they often wondered about each other.

After parting from Kate, Malcolm was still very much missing her and wishing he could have stayed with her a little longer, but time schedules had to be kept. Malcolm had a very important meeting with some of the townspeople and looked forward to talking about the situation that had currently developed. Driving back toward town, he could see that Ian was hard at work pounding out the metal of someone's order as the clank of hammer on steel echoed from the forge clear out to the road which passed by the forge. The area was bustling with people going about their daily routines and conducting their chores, from the roadside stands of fresh produce to tinsmithswho displayed their noisy wares of pots and pans and other kitchen utensils. Along the way were many cottages with neatly trimmed yards, thatched roofs, and stone walls painted white.As Malcolm continued on down the road toward the heart of Forfar, herds of Highland Coos would block the road as they made their way to the next pasture land to graze. The church Malcolm attended and where he was to meet the others was just outside the center of town, not too far from the main hustle and bustle of activities. The church sat on a small mound of ground that kept it from flooding when the local creek rose.The creek had done this on several occasions, but the church had yet to suffer any water damage.

Malcolm pulled his carriage up to the front of the church where several other carriages and horses were tied. He noticed some of the men congregating in the front of the double doors at the entrance of the church. Some of the men were good friends of Malcolm's, others were mostly acquaintances, and some he didn't know at all. Petting his horse on the nose and making sure he was calm, Malcolm made his way to the entrance to greet his companions.

"Hello, Malcolm," said Kenneth MacOmish, a local landowner who raised cattle just north of Forfar.

"And a good day to you, Kenneth. Good to see you again, Scott, David," Malcolm replied.

"I don't believe you know George Ferguson or Kevin Howard, Malcolm. George just recently became a member of our congregation, and Howard is fairly new to the area also," Kenneth told Malcolm.

Shaking the hands of both George Ferguson and Kevin Howard, Malcolm was pleased to make their acquaintance. Kenneth MacOmish and Scott Weems were old friends with Malcolm and had grown up with him in Forfar. They had attended church together most of their lives even before the present church had been built. They had seen the area grow up around them and lived through many changes that had occurred over their lifetimes. David MacDougall had moved to the area later in Malcolm's life, but he too had become a good friend to him through the years. George was too new for Malcolm to have gotten to know, but he had seen him around town and in church. "Well, let's go inside where we can be more comfortable and have a talk," Kenneth said.

The church was very spacious inside and was ornately decorated as any church of the time would be. Many religious artifacts and symbols adorned the walls and vestibule area with the pews all neatly formed in rows with one main aisle. Ornate carvings along the upper ceiling showed some of the history of Forfar as well as the saints mentioned in the Bible. Even stories from various books of the Bible were displayed for all to ponder as they sat and reflected upon their faith. Malcolm and his friends made their way to an open conference area to conduct their business. As the men all took seats around the table, Kenneth thanked everyone for coming to support Malcolm.

"I called this meeting to reach out to our friend, Malcolm, whom I have known for many years, as some of you have also, and to show our support for him and his son. Malcolm has come under fire recently through no fault of his own by people who wish him harm. I, for one, and I'm sure you men too just by being here, am not going to allow one of our own to fall prey to vicious attacks and stand by and do nothing," Kenneth said.

"Here! Here!" Scott Weems said. "I feel the same way and will do whatever it takes to make Malcolm feel safe until we catch the hoodlums responsible for the attacks that have taken place in our community."

"Malcolm, we are all united to lend a hand to do whatever we can to make you feel secure and safe. Why, if we have to, we'll stand guard over your house at night while you sleep," David MacDougall said.

"Okay, okay, I get the message, but I don't need you hovering over me like a hen with chicks! I do appreciate your help and concern, but you all have families and businesses to attend to also. Ian and I will be just fine, especially with good neighbors like you around," Malcolm said.

"Let me discuss something that recently came my way," Kenneth said. "I was doing some legal deed checking concerning the adjacent land next to mine in hopes of buying it up since Old Man MacGregor was getting up in years and was thinking of moving to Edinburgh to live with relatives there."

"He is getting along, isn't he? It's been awhile since I've even seen him in church, poor guy," Malcolm said.

"Yes, well, I've made him a proposal that's a fair price, and I would love to add his property to mine. I could use the additional acres for my cattle, which are growing right out from under me. But here's what concerns me about all this: Mr. Weems here and Mr. Ferguson found strange information concerning the deed that Mr. MacGregor held. It seems that although Walter MacGregor has lived on this property for all these many years, he was not the outright owner of the property," Kenneth said.

"Well, why didn't MacGregor buy the land after all these years? Most people want to own outright the land they work," Malcolm said. "You would assume that, but you would be wrong. Of course, there is land that is leased and rented out to crofters, which is apparently, by legal terms, what MacGregor was doing," Kenneth said.

"That's right. By law he was paying rent to the real owner either in labor or goods rendered," Scott interjected.

"So how is he to move away without any money to survive on after all these years?" Malcolm asked.

"That I wouldn't know. Maybe he saved up all these years. Maybe his relatives in Edinburgh are going to pay for his keep," Scott said. "From what I heard, he doesn't have any relatives left," Malcolm said.

The others sitting around the table were taking it all in as Malcolm, Scott, and Kenneth had the floor. George, being a banker, understood the financial aspects of loans and interest. David MacDougall, being in the general merchandise business, had a good head for buying and selling everyday items of need. Kevin Howard, well, no one really understood what opinion he might have on this subject seeing that he was a poet and painter of landscapes. Malcolm thought one of the men here must have known enough about Kevin to invite him to this meeting; maybe Kevin had ideas but was too shy or didn't feel comfortable talking in front of people he wasn't that familiar with. Malcolm did notice though that he had a ring on his left hand that was truly unique with a design Malcolm had never seen before. He wanted to ask him about it, but thought better of it. "Well, I can tell you who the land is registered to if anyone's interested. A Theodore Higginbottom. Name mean anything to anyone here?" Scott asked.

Malcolm nearly fell out of his seat at the mention of that name. "Did you say . . . Higginbottom? Theodore Higginbottom?"Malcolm said with a tinge of trepidation. He felt the blood drain from his head, and his breathing became deeper as his heart beat faster. How could that man's influence still be generating feelings of fear and anger after so long ago? It was though, and Malcolm got a real jolt of it just now.

"I don't know how much any of you know about my family and the relationship that the current events play in that, but this Higginbottom fellow is at the core of those events. I don't want to go too deeply into my family history, but maybe it's just a coincidence that he is the owner of the property and that he is probably responsible for the attacks here in the region," Malcolm said.

Malcolm saw the look on the faces of the men at the table when he made his statement, and most of them wore shocked expressions except Kevin. He just looked down at his hands without making any gestures or showing any emotion at all.

"Malcolm, are you sure it's the same man? Maybe someone with a similar sounding name or maybe . . . ?" Kenneth said.

"Or maybe what? No one who is a respectable landowner would allow the use of their property to be associated with a group like this. How could someone living in our community be a party to this kind of activity?" Malcolm said.

"I will go over the books again just to make sure of our facts," said Scott.

"My father was killed by this man and his colleagues, and apparently, his kind are still out here roaming the countryside stirring up the same type of mischief," Malcolm said.

"Is Mr. Falconer working the case?" David Macdougall asked."He is, but like he says, he only has so many men to patrol the whole area. I'm sure he's doing all he can. I have seen several of his constables not far from my cottage on occasion, so it looks like he's doing what he said. I have several other fellows watching out for me as well," Malcolm said.

"Where is this . . . Higginbottom now? Why don't we have the magistrate go and arrest him if he's the guilty party?" Kevin finally spoke up.

"Because he's in the colonies, clear across the ocean where he ran many years ago. He was responsible for the witch hunts here in Forfar and killed many innocent people then. Apparently, he kept his property and holdings and never sold out. He must have an overseer to mind his business for him while he is abroad," Malcolm said.

"Well, are there other relatives of the Higginbottom family who might be connected to his holdings here?" Mr. Ferguson asked. "In our title searches we went back through the deeds and found that there are other Higginbottom names we assume are related, but they live in England," Scott said.

"Mr. Higginbottom's family is originally from England, I believe near London if memory serves me," Kenneth added.

All of a sudden, Malcolm didn't feel comfortable talking about this subject any longer. The mood of the meeting seemed to suggest to Malcolm that enough had been said. He had a feeling of distrust and disloyalty being harbored. "If it's all the same to you men, I need to get back to my forge. I've left Ian alone for most of the day, and I don't want to get behind. I do thank you all for your support though and know you have my best interests at heart. Thank you once again," Malcolm concluded.

"If you need anything—anything— just let us know. We'll be there for you," Kenneth said.

"That goes for all of us. That's what community is for, watching out for your neighbor," Scott said.

As Malcolm said his good-byes, he made his way out to his carriage and gave a carrot to his horse before he boarded. "Good ole Thunder, you've waited patiently for me, haven't you, boy?" Climbing up into the seat, Malcolm turned his carriage around and headed for home. The streets were still very busy as Malcolm nodded to those whom he passed. In a slow, lazy trot, Malcolm made his way down the road, tipping his hat to Mrs. Williams as she strolled by some of the shops, waving to Mr. Henderson sweeping his storefront area to make it more presentable to customers. He wondered who was truly his friend and who was simply masquerading as his friend to catch him unaware at a weak moment. It made him suspicious of everyone he saw and this was not the way Malcolm wanted to behave. He knew he had good, trustworthy friends, people whom he had known for years in the community, who helped him and whom he had helped in the past. These were people whom he would die for under the right circumstance, people he had grown up with and had attended weddings and funerals with. He was not going to turn his back on the many just to avoid the few. He was going to trust his friends and his instincts to get to the bottom of this ordeal.

The next day, Malcolm decided that he was going to let Ian sleep in. He was up at the crack of dawn and headed toward the forge to fire it up and get the day started. Ian had done a great job of keeping up with the customers' orders, and this made Malcolm feel like he truly had a partner in the business. Ian was someone whom he could count on to fill in and take up any slack when Malcolm was drawn away onother business. Today, he was back in the forge and feeling good about the day and looking forward to meeting his clients and customers. He knew Ian would be up soon and, as usual, making his enormous breakfast. As soon as Ian joined him at the forge, Malcolm would go back in and have a bowl of porridge and some fresh milk for his breakfast. With all the swords being made lately, one would think there was a clan war getting ready to break out. Actually, there was always a skirmish or feud going on, so this was not so unrealistic at all. Although Forfar was just outside the Highland line, it still saw plenty of kilted Highlanders who came out of the hills to conduct business like everyone else. Those who lived further in the mountains would do without before mingling with city folk. Of course, they wouldn't turn down some of the more conventional things that others would bring back to them, but they just wouldn't make the trip themselves. Life in the Highlands was not an easy life. The ground was at times hard and even impossible to plow. Other clans would steal cattle, which would be a big part of the year's income.

The weather was horrible most of the time, especially in winter, which meant that simple shelter was essential for day-to-day survival. Thatched roofs and dirt floors did not provide a lot of insulation. Cattle were even housed in some homes, not only for protecting the beasts, but for the more practical idea of providing warmth for the occupants. Sometimes, the only opportunity to leave the Highlands was when they would drive their cattle to the southern markets in the border area or even into England itself. Most Highlanders spent their whole life in the Highlands and knew no other way but the Highland way.

Malcolm was, for the most part, a happy and contented man. Other than not having his wife around like he once had, he did very well. Now that Kate was becoming a regular and important part of his life, he was finding that he wanted for nothing at this point. He tried to stay humble and never pretentious as he dealt with people every day. He was thankful for what he had acquired and achieved in life. Yes, he was a happy man.

After Ian joined Malcolm for the day's work, they both put in a hard morning and completed many of the orders they had promised to customers. Malcolm's reputation was almost becoming a problem in that people would come from many, many miles away to have him make a weapon for them. It was almost more than he could handle. He knew for sure that without Ian, he would never be able to do it all. "Ian, I have to go visit the magistrate and see what progress he's made with our case. Finish up with the Grant order and call it a day, Son. We're far enough ahead to allow for some time off to enjoy the fruits of our labor."

Malcolm pulled off his torn and dirty apron and hung it on a peg by the door. He took a clean rag from the bin and began rubbing the soot off his arms, neck, and face, finishing up with lye soap and water from the trough on the opposite side of the door. Finally, drying off his body with one of the clean towels from the bin, he was ready to at last present himself in a reasonable manner in town.

The drive back into town went quickly, for he had a lot of things on his mind that he might ask the magistrate. He wanted to find out if the magistrate had made any progress on locating the people responsible for the murders and the threats made against him. At the Tolbooth, Malcolm hitched his horse to the post and walked into the building where the officials were located.

"Good afternoon, Magistrate Falconer."

"And to you too, Mr. MacGow. I suppose you want to know about the current case, if I don't miss my guess?" "Aye, and to thank you for the added protection near my cottage. We've had no incidents since you've been watching out for us." "Excellent! I'm glad that's worked out for both of us. I can tell you that we have gathered some evidence, but I also have to tell you that it has disappeared," Mr. Falconer said.

"Disappeared? What do you mean? You had evidence, but it's gone now?" Malcolm said with a disillusioned tone. "What kind of evidence?"

"We discovered what we think is a group of people who are part of an organization that are actually occultists, devil worshipers." "Devil worshipers? Here in Forfar?" Malcolm asked.

"That is correct. Two of my constables caught a group of men near the spot where the Druid was hanged during some sort of ritual. As we approached, they ran in different directions, but we did manage to catch up to one of them. When we captured him, he started mumbling something about, 'a great blue Deva of the First ray— you have to let me finish— I must complete this.' I have no idea what he was referring to.It just sounded crazy to me," Magistrate Falconer said."You mentioned something about lost evidence. What was the evidence?" Malcolm asked.

"Well, I'm assuming it was evidence. It was a . . . kind of napkin- no more than that; it was like an apron of sorts, you might say, with strange symbols embroidered on it. We took it from the captured fellow."

"So what happened to the apron and where is the captured fellow? Has he said anymore?" Malcolm asked.

"The apron is nowhere to be found. The fellow in question . . . well, he died while in custody. We found him dead in his cell below, of natural causes I guess you would say. No marks on him, but his eyes were open when we found him yesterday morning."

"This all sounds too unbelievable, Mr. Falconer. Doesn't it sound strange to you that the only possible suspect has died and the evidence has disappeared?" Malcolm said.

"We find it very disturbing, I can assure you, Mr. MacGow, but we're trying to get to the bottom of it. There's something I want to show you that I think you will find interesting." Following the magistrate and one of his constables into the office, Malcolm watched as Mr. Falconer retrieved a map from one of the closets in his office. He spread it out on one of the tables and smoothed down the edges so it didn't roll back in its tube form.

"This is a map of Forfar and some of the surrounding area of our lands. Look here on the western side; you'll see where your property lies. Here's the area north of here where Mr. MacGregor's property lies, and here on the eastern side is where they held the witch trials some thirty years ago," Mr. Falconer said.

"And what's this circle in the center here?" Malcolm asked. "Well, if you draw a line from your place to MacGregor's to the witch trial area, what do you see?" Mr. Falconer asked Malcolm. "It's a sort of triangle design. Is there some significance to that? And what is the circle in the middle?"

"The circle in the middle is the Tolbooth which we are now currently occupying." As Malcolm studied the map a little more, tryingto make sense of it all, the constable started to gather up the map to place it back in the closet. As he folded the map back into a tubular shape, Malcolm's eye caught a glimpse of his hands and noticed the ring on his finger and tried to remember where he'd seen that design before. It reminded Malcolm of a lightning bolt of sorts, maybe an 's' design; no it was more like a lightning bolt, Malcolm thought to himself. Where had he seen that before?

"So you see, Malcolm, it's kind of odd, concerning that shape on the map, that triangle I mean. Do you think it means anything?" Mr. Falconer asked Malcolm.

"To me it doesn't. I haven't a clue. Why is my forge connected to the design? Is that significant?"

"We're still investigating. We just don't have enough information yet."

"I'm going to do a little investigating myself. I know I said I would let you do all the checking and investigating, but I can maybe do something to help. I'll be in touch with you if I find out anything," Malcolm said.

Malcolm racked his brain to remember where he had seen the lightning bolt design as he left the Tolbooth. Before he mounted his carriage, he looked up and down the street to see if he knew anyone he might want to say hello to, but no one he knew was in sight. He decided to walk a bit and maybe visit some of the shops that he normally didn't have time to look in. He came to a clothing shop first and noticed some of the fashions displayed in the window and thought them to be more English-inspired than anything normally found in Scotland. He knew that the English had a definite influence on things in Scotland because they had basically bribed the Scots with their trinkets of fashion and all the high times of London aristocracy so they could gain a foothold into Scottish life and politics. Unfortunately, the Scots were prone to the temptations of wanting those things as if they really needed them. They couldn't say no to them. The English knew this too. They always had the carrot to wave in front of them to entice them toward the south and to intermingle their culture with the Scottish. Always they offered promises of a better way of life while trying to entice them to give up their own culture. The English got control, but not always by military might.

As Malcolm made his way on down the street, he happened to glance back toward the Tolbooth and noticed the constable who had been in the room with him, standing outside the door. Malcolm thought he saw him looking at him and then suddenly look away when Malcolm glanced his direction. He thought for sure that the constable was watching him.

Malcolm decided to pick up some fish that was on display across the street and headed that way. He thought he would surprise Ian and treat him to some fresh seafood for dinner tonight. Of course, he would let Ian prepare it since Ian could do a far better job in the food department than he could. But he was sure Ian wouldn't mind; after all, fish was a treat. Ian loved fish, even better than steak. Malcolm guessed that the smell of the salt air blowing in had made Ian crave seafood more than beef. Either way though, Ian could cook it to its most savory conclusion. That's exactly what he did that night. He threw in some bannocks—some called them oatcakes— a few scones with scotch broth, and some crowdies. Of course, they washed it down with some good whisky, which Malcolm just happened to have on hand.

"Well, Ian, what can I say to the best cook in the house? You've done it again! Of course I did catch the fish, you know," Malcolm kidded Ian.

"Then why were they wrapped in paper when you came home?" Ian asked.

"Yeah, you got me. But they were fresh, you have to admit," Malcolm said.

"By the way, I'm having trouble with the ring attachments on the tack of 'Old Lightning' right where the bridle fits into the harness on the . . ."

"What did you just say?"

"The tack is not . . ."

"No, you said the ring and then lightning . . . That's where I saw the symbol on the constable's ring—on Mr. Howard's at the church. They have the same ring with the same insignia. A lightning bolt on their rings. What're the odds of that?" Malcolm asked.

Thirteen

The village that Daniel and Adam were led to was quite impressive. The houses were close to two-hundred feet long and capable of housing many people under one roof. There were many people in the village and it looked like a small city that had sprung up in the wilderness. Women were scurrying about with baskets under their arms while others held small children as older ones clung to their mothers like calves to cows. They were all curious to see the strangers that had just entered their village, especially Adam. This occasion of Druids and Indian peoples mixing was bringing Adam to an emotional state that Daniel had never witnessed. It was most disturbing to Adam.

In the village, there seemed to be no one who didn't have something to do. They all were working diligently, moving about in a very busy activity. A few dogs ran after each other, barking and nipping, declaring their territory. Being near the river, there were canoes docked along the bank. Some were coming to shore while others were moving into the middle of the currents to head to their next destination. This was a village with much commerce going on. Daniel was used to this type of arrangement in the village setting as he had dealt with the Indians for a few years now in his hunting and trading. He had become familiar with their language and knew how to bargain with them— how to strike a good deal so that each party felt they had gotten the best part of the transaction. Daniel never felt like he was walking away the poorer of the two.

It was hard to figure how far they had marched since they didn't stop too often for any reason on the way to the village. It was a forced march that took up a lot of time and miles, but got them to their destination as planned. Daniel still did not know what their agenda was in this part of the colonies.

"We are glad you chose to come with us on our trek here to the village. We are honored to have you both as guests," said the Frenchman.

"You still haven't told us why you have brought us here—against our will, by the way," Daniel said. "Why are the French so far inland? You do know you're in British territory?"

"Ah, monsieur, you worry about imaginary boundaries. We mean no one any harm."

Daniel watched as pack animals were also coming and going in the village. They were laden down with heavy packs as they made their way beyond the village and into the woods. They were led by other Frenchmen while the Iroquois marched beside them. It was a steady stream of activity with all the animals coming and going and boats docking and shoving off.This was not a normal day for any Iroquois. As the procession passed by, one of the mules got spooked and started bucking. As the mule kicked first to the right and then to the left, the French guide tried his best to hold the reins and to bring the animal under control. In the process, one of the bags burst loose and spilled its contents on the ground.

"Gems!" Daniel exclaimed. "There must be a fortune just lying on the ground in front of us, Adam."

"I have seen many precious stones in my time, but if all these bags are stuffed like this one, it would be impossible to count them all," Adam concluded.

"This must have been a forward party surveying the area for possibly more treasure. We were just unfortunate to have been in their path. They wanted to keep us silent so they brought us with them," Daniel said. "They have certainly hit upon a major find, that's for sure. My guess would be that somehow the French found out that the Iroquois had discovered the gems, probably through just seeing them wear them around their necks and arms, and recognized a source of possible wealth. They struck some sort of deal with them, which brings us to this point," Daniel concluded.

"Sounds logical. You think that's all there is to it?" Adam asked.

"Don't really know, but I do believe that gems mean different things to different people. To the Indians, they're just trinkets that shine, but to Europeans, they're riches," Daniel said."Apparently, they are hauling them into the village and transporting them up river to French territory at some point. The only problem is that the British are the rightful owners of the gems, but they do not know about the find. How ironic. The French do not know that I couldn't tell the British if I wanted to, seeing that I'm hunted by them for prison escape, and you could care less," Daniel said.

As several Iroquois came running to pick up the gems and secure them in another sack, the Frenchman saw that Daniel and Adam had witnessed the accident.

"Monsieur, you see that we are astute businessmen like yourselves, I'm sure. We have an agreement with our Indian brothers that make both sides happy, you see. We can put these stones to far better use than they, and in return, we fight off their enemies for them. Of course, we supply them with the best weapons we have, so they can defend themselves. Surely you can see our predicament. We could not have these beautiful rocks just wasting away here in this desolate wilderness. We simply became 'aware' of them and acted appropriately, you see."

"Monsieur, we are not your enemy. We could care less about your little expedition. We have our own problems and concerns and simply want to be on our way. Could you not see yourself clear to allow us to leave?" Daniel pleaded.

"We could, but we are on a time schedule which we can't afford to have interrupted. We must complete our mission here, and I'm sure then you will be on your way."

"What is the time schedule? How long must we remain here?"

"Again, we cannot say. But I can assure you it is near. Far too many like yourself are venturing out this way, whether exploring or hunting and trapping. We must finish this and be on our way. I can say only that it will be days, not weeks. Please be patient."

Adam was not a happy man with the circumstances. He felt weak and uninspired to act. His magic was truly being affected by the close proximity to the Indian population. Daniel had never understood how the Druids operated. He just knew they were special and possessed strengths and abilities that most men did not. Daniel thought that Adam was suffering from what he believed was his Achilles heel. Whether real or perceived, Adam was out of sorts. Daniel wanted not just to get free himself, but he wanted Adam back to his old self. Adam thought to himself that he was not going to be a good guest to the French.

"What have we to report regarding our Daniel MacGow, Mr. Bryson?" Mr. Higginbottom asked. Mr. Jack Bryson was head of special security for Theodore Higginbottom and was the best in the colonies at running bodyguard details and protecting whomever he was assigned to. He had been brought over some time after Mr. Higginbottom had arrived and set up his next venture of witch hunts in America. Mr. Bryson had worked all over England, spying on people who were not external enemies of England, but of a different political party or opinion of those who were in office or trying to get into office. He had been responsible for more than a few assassinations in his time and would do whatever he was hired to do. He was underhanded and could be bought for a price. He was the best at what he did. He took it personally that Daniel had not only escaped from his men but had even killed a few of them. He was not giving up, just regrouping.

"Daniel MacGow is temporarily a free man, Your Grace, but he will be captured in due time, I swear."

"How is it that one man has eluded you and your force? Isn't he nothing more than a trapper?" Mr. Higginbottom asked.

"He was not alone, Your Grace. He had three other men with him that fought like ten men. We managed to kill two, but Daniel and his companion fled into the wilderness. We could not pursue as we were getting dangerously close to Indian lands and could find ourselves surrounded and outnumbered.I did post two men within shouting distance of each other in case they returned. With your permission, I'd like to go after our prey alone. I believe that I could skirt the Indian population, go unnoticed and pick up the trail of MacGow once more. It would be easier to go unnoticed with just myself to worry about," Mr. Bryson said.

"Maybe the Indians have finished them off for us already. I would hate to not be able to see Daniel die in person but, anyway, you have my permission to go. At this point, dead or alive, doesn't matter. You will be amply rewarded if you succeed; if you fail, you will be shipped back to England on the first boat outbound, without your titles, of course. I will see you as a front line soldier in the King's army fighting in a hell-hole in some God-forsaken country," Mr. Higginbottom pronounced.

Jack Bryson knew that Higginbottom would do just as he said. Failure was not an option for him now. He had to succeed or become as nothing from that moment on. The stakes were high since he enjoyed his lifestyle very much. He had gained much fortune through the years and had invested wisely. If he were to fail, it would be better to simply disappear rather than face Higginbottom. He would not be going back to simple soldiering. That would be worse than death for him. He was going to find MacGow if it did indeed kill him.

Mr. Theodore Higginbottom stayed dutifully focused on persecuting witches; at least that was what everyone thought he was doing. Protecting the good people from the evil influence of the Devil's disciples was his calling. He was commissioned by the powers that be to stamp out this demonic influence in the Massachusetts colony and bring Christianity to the forefront of their society.What people didn't stop to think about was that no one had really noticed any witch activity until Mr. Higginbottom came on the scene; coincidence or timely intervention?

"Is the meeting place all set for tonight, Mr. Dodsworth?" Mr. Higginbottom asked.

"That it is, sir. All will be in order."

The monthly meeting of the Sacred Cross was tonight. Only special people who were initiated into this group could attend or even know it existed. They were a secretive bunch who didn't talk about their organization, but remained very close to one another and looked after each other in everyday business and general life.

They were one of many such groups that existed all over the world. Their names were usually different, but they all shared the same goals.They preached world brotherhood where men were supposed to live together in peace and harmony. They took sacred oaths and swore allegiance to their cause and each other. They tried to achieve their goals any way they could, including murder if that was necessary. They believed they were superior to most people, and so whatever it took to reach their ambitious dreams or desired results was legal. They looked upon human law as fit only for the masses— beneath them. They were setting up society to become what they envisioned it should be for their master whom they worshiped. They saw it no other way. They felt that the one they worshiped was the strongest and that he would reward them in the end. They sought power, riches and position over those below them— the unenlightened.

As the sun was going down, the local folks began to close down their businesses and shops for the day. Some were collecting their goods that had been on display throughout the day and bringing their wares indoors. Some had had a good day, some not so good, but tomorrow would be another day. Doors were locked, and the shop owners would begin their journey home for supper and family time. Others would stay just a little longer at their place of business to possibly catch the last few stragglers that might make their day successful. Some of them had no one to go home to and lived a lonely kind of life with only tomorrow to look forward to. But there were some who had an agenda that they couldn't wait to embrace. They were people who were the upper crust of society that had privilege and viewed themselves as elite. They ran high-end businesses that garnished huge profits and didn't have to scrape the bottom of the economic barrel. They ran most of society that was of importance. They were set apart from the rest simply by the way they dressed. Some of these people would be attending a special meeting tonight.

Night had fallen, and most of the residents had taken shelter for the night. There were a few still out on horseback and a few still on foot making their way to their destinations. Some were in carriages going to a house that was hard to see from the road because it sat way back on the property, hidden from the casual eye by trees and shrubbery. This house was the home of Theodore Higginbottom, who especially savored his privacy and locked himself away from everyday life on his very own island with a mysterious secret. Tonight, they all would be calling upon the name of The Great Architect of the Universe.

Fourteen

Malcolm realized that he was very deep in this whole mystery and that his family played a big part whether they were here or abroad. He was determined to protect his family and his family name from attacks by either man or devil. He hadn't asked for this fight nor was he looking for it when it came his way, but now that he was in it, he aimed to see it through. His Highland blood had been bought and paid for by his ancestors, and he was not going to let any of them down. If only these adversaries would face him man to man with sword in hand. After Malcolm had filled Ian in on the details of the day's activities, they had planned on relaxing around the fireplace reading or telling tales about their Scottish lineage. Stories were usually passed down from each generation and told in an oral manner. The Scots were great storytellers. They would usually involve personal family history, whether for good deeds or black ones, but told they were. Malcolm was about to tell one to Ian as they reclined and sprawled by the nice, warm fire that blazed so high they couldn't see the top of the flames. Ian had built this one to last through the night.

"Ian, have I ever told you about your grandfather's trip to Breamarin the Cairngorm Mountains?"

"No, sir, you haven't," Ian said.

"It was back before I was even born, I believe in 1645, as the story goes. Father had gone there by request of the twelfth Earl of Mar to make a special sword for him. Robert's reputation as a fine sword maker had reached the Earl, and so Father made the trip there. He spent several weeks there, was treated like royalty and was paid well also. The Earl was pleased with the sword, but never got a chance to use it for he died a few years later. While there though, the other blacksmith and several other townspeople were having a friendly game, and a wager developed. The game stemmed around who could toss a hammer the farthest out in the field from the forge. As Robert was new in town and the local blacksmith was a bit miffed over not being asked to make the sword, Robert was challenged to compete to see what he was made of. Robert was really not interested, but they kept egging him on, and so to save face, he accepted. It seems that the hammer was some twenty-two inches long and weighed about ten stones. Well, the first man gripped the hammer and swung it around his head several times and let go finally to see it travel about eighteen meters or so. They thought that not a bad throw. The next man, much bigger and apparently stronger, swung it around his head a few times and released it in front of him to a distance of about twenty meters, beating the first man. Father, watching the techniques of the first two men and never having thrown a hammer before, decided that there was a better way. He could see that throwing the hammer and releasing it to the front caused the men to lose a lot of power. Robert took hold of the hammer and put his back to the target area and than began his swing motion. He swung three times in a circle above his head and released the hammer over his shoulder, not able to see where it was headed. After regaining his balance, he turned to see his throw travel a distance of some thirty-three meters, beating both of his opponents. They stood there with mouths wide open and jaws to their knees in disbelief. One of them said that the throw was illegal because of the way he had thrown, but Father reminded them that they had stated no such rules, and he won the wager. Father refused the prize but said that he would return next year, and they could try to beat him then."

"Did he return the next year?" Ian asked.

"From what I understand, he did, and they made it a yearly event for several years after. I had the opportunity to go with Father on two of the trips when I was very small. Father was eventually defeated because others began throwing like he did and were a little stronger. They actually developed several other events to go with the hammer throw, but I never returned after awhile, so I don't know if they are still doing them or not."

"Grandfather was quite a man, wasn't he?" Ian asked. "I'm glad I got to know him for the time I did before his death."

"He was quite a man. I miss him a lot." Malcolm's mind began to wander concerning his father and how he had died by the hands of the same people who were quite possibly trying to kill him too. He longed for the peace and quiet that he had experienced before.He went over all the happenings from beginning to end, including the coincidence of the matching rings on the two local men. Was it merely a coincidence that they both had the same ring design? He just didn't know. And what about the triangle design on the map in the Magistrate's office, the one that included his own property?

"I'm turning in, Dad. Had a rough day and can't keep my eyes open any longer," Ian announced.

"Okay, good night, son. See you in the morning."

As Ian went off to bed, Malcolm folded his arms under the back of his neck and stared at the ceiling, still contemplating tomorrow and his date with Kate. He was glad she was in his life to break the tension and strain of what he was going through lately. She was so beautifuland loving toward him, and he longed for her all the time. She had the lips of an angel, he thought, and he couldn't wait to kiss her again. He would often relate to her his wishes, but she would say, "Don't wishfor what you want; do something about it." He tried to live by her words. He had learned so much from her in the short time they had been together. He tried to make her happy as best he could and proclaimed his undying love for her whenever they were together. If she learned anything from him, it was that he loved her with every fiber in his being.

As he started to drift off to sleep, he thought he heard the pecking of a bird, maybe a woodpecker, or some other animal clawing at his house. He didn't know if it was the start of a dream or reality. Maybe a branch scraping the side of the house in the wind. There it was again; it was a tapping on his windowpane. He jostled himself awake and looked toward the sound at the window. There was a figure he couldn't make out, and it gave him a start that made him jump. He rolled over on his side, keeping his eyes on the person outside his window. A Druid! He recognized the cowl of the cape over his head. Was it one he had already met before or someone new? He went to the door. "Who is it?"

"I am Louis Mar. I come in the name of the Druid Society. May I see you?"

Malcolm opened the door as the Druid quickly stepped inside and closed the door. He threw the hood of his cape back to reveal his face. True enough, Malcolm thought to himself, I don't know him. "What brings you out at this late hour?"

"It is safer if we meet this way as many unfriendly people are out and about this hour. You were very busy all day, and I couldn't chance being seen with you in the daylight hours."

"Have you been watching this house very long? I was told the Druid brotherhood would keep an eye out for us."

"And that we have. We know you went to the Tolbooth today and we know that one of the constables is watching you, but not for your protection. You cannot trust him. We are well aware of who is looking out for your good and who is not. The Enlightened Ones are here in this town and countryside. You must be very careful where you go and whom you see. You should not go alone."

"Some very unusual happenings occurred today that have really got me thinking. Do you know about the MacGregor house and its connection to Mr. Higginbottom? Do you know about the triangle of properties? The lightning bolt rings, the . . ."

"We know. We have for many years been studying these people, and our people have fought them for hundreds of years. We know them well, Malcolm MacGow, very well."

"I'm glad you do. For awhile I thought I was going crazy with conspiracy thoughts. Then it's true, there is something to all these going ons that are real and dangerous. What has our property to dowith the triangle?"

"This area was chosen a long time ago for Druid practices. When our people first came to this area, we knew that the strength of the land here was right for our rituals. The Picts were here and allowed us to co-mingle with them without upsetting either of our daily routines."

"The Picts . . . the ancient people who painted themselves blue when they went into battle?" Malcolm queried.

"That is correct. They were in Scotland before the nation was called Scotland. They disappeared into history somehow, maybe assimilated themselves with other people or just left. The Scots from Ireland also came here, and eventually all the people became one nation under McAlpine," the Druid explained.

"The forces were very strong here in this area," he continued, "and it's why we were led here and stayed.Have you ever noticed the enormous rock on your property about thirty meters behind your forge?"

"I am well aware of that rock. We were never able to move it, so we just left it where it stood and built around it. My father said it was there when he was a boy.We just ignore it for the most part. Weused to jump off of it when we were smaller and played around it all the time," Malcolm said.

"Well, what's unusual about this rock is there are two other ones exactly like it in the area. Want to guess where they are?"

"Two other ones . . . the triangle!" Malcolm guessed.

"Correct again. One is on the MacGregor farm and the other at the place of the witch trials. They form a triangle which our people used in the rituals we performed because of the strength and energy that flowed in the area."

"On the map I also noticed a circle right near the middle of the triangle where the Tolbooth sits today," Malcolm noted.

"The Tolbooth is where my people, a long time ago, had their temple. I'm sure there are evidences of that in the basement of the Tolbooth hidden behind walls or in the ground. There have to be post-holes or pits where my people performed their duties and rituals. I have never been able to go there since it belongs to the authorities, which is unfortunate."

"When I was down there, looking at the body of the Druid who was killed, I could feel strange things in the air that made my skin crawl, and it was all I could do to just stand there. There were other passages and doors that I have no idea where they might go. You don't want to be imprisoned there. It's a hellish place," Malcolm concluded. "I could gather so much from that holy ground if I could but visit it. There are probably artifacts that would be so helpful in piecing together my past history. It would be a rich find for me."

"So what better place to build a blacksmith shop than on holy Druid ground?" Malcolm said.

"As you well know, Druids and blacksmiths have worked together since the beginning of time. They have been brothers to us for as long as there have been Druids. Smiths have erected monuments of stone and must have had a part in the making of Stonehenge in England and the Callanish stones in the Hebrides," the Druid spoke.

"So the rocks on the other two places are the same material, and there is no other rock like them in the area. That would suggest that the rocks had to have been carried here from somewhere else. True?"

"Right again, but even my history doesn't tell me from where. I do know this: the stones at Stonehenge are the same type as the ones here. This might suggest that they at least came from the same area."

"But now these areas, except for mine, are in the hands of someone who is not friendly toward your kind or mine as well. Do you still feel the magic of the area or has it died?" Malcolm asked.

"It has dwindled through time, but it's still a sacred place to us. Many memories can still be relived and used in our practice. As long as one MacGow remains alive, we will be here to protect you. This we have vowed. Although we as Druids have lost most of our true culture to the Romanization of Europe and Britain, we still survive with whatever is remembered and practiced. We remain true to what we know.When we are all gone, my hope is that our influence will continue in the lives of others in some lasting way," Louis Mar said."I find it hard to believe that the Enlightened Ones are simply holding a grudge against me and my family after all these years. Surely not?" Malcolm asked.

"It is not just a grudge, Malcolm. They want your land and the stone. They want to complete ownership of the four areas in question to control the sites for their purposes. They are an unholy band, but they believe in what they are doing. You have to remember that this group has been practicing their art for many years as well. It may be a new name with a new group of converts, but it's the same old mission of world conquest for their leader."

"They want us out, off of our land that has been in our family for generations?"

"They want you all dead so that no one can lay claim to it later as well. Your brother, Daniel, in the colonies, is a target I'm sure. That's why we have our Druid people there as well. My father is one of those Druids."

As the night wore on, Louis Mar concluded his business with Malcolm. The Druid slipped out of the house into the night shadows and disappeared like mist dissolving in the air.

Malcolm got only minimal sleep, but still awoke before Ian. But Ian wasn't far behind him, just more refreshed. As Ian prepared breakfast for two, Malcolm filled him in on the nightly visitor and all they had talked about. Ian was attentive as he cooked and almost burned the oatcakes as his mind was on the Druid visit. Even his burned oatcakes were better than most people's. After a hearty breakfast, both men were on their way to the forge to pound out steel into the desired shapes. It didn't take long for them to get dirty with grease and soot over their arms and faces. Anyone could easily identify them as blacksmiths with their occupational warpaint. It turned out to be a very busy day at the forge, but Malcolm was still going to make room for Kate this afternoon. Kate had planned on taking a drive with Malcolm to a neighboring town and treating him to a nice lunch. Malcolm was turning the reins over to Ian once again so Malcolm could keep his date. Ian actually enjoyed it when Malcolm would go on his "business trips," because it left him in charge and he wanted to be the one who was running the forge, at least for a little while.

"Ian, I will be home a little later, at least in time for supper. If you run into anything you can't handle, I'll tend to it tomorrow."

"I'll handle it, Dad. Have I ever had a problem at blacksmithing that I haven't handled?" Ian asked.

"Well, there was the situation of the sword for Mr. Clark that you made so heavy that even you couldn't lift it without using both hands." "What's wrong with carrying a sword with two hands?" Ian asked in a perplexed tone.

"Because the sword was to be a present for his daughter on her eighteenth birthday. She couldn't have lifted it if she had had four hands." Malcolm gave a slight snicker.

"Okay, I'll give you that one, but we did sell it to her older brother who loved it.Besides, I've come a long way since then, haven't I?" "I'm just giving you a hard time, Ian. I trust you completely." After cleaning up and putting on a clean shirt, Malcolm dusted his kilt off and headed to his rendezvous with Kate, the love of his life. They met at a market place called Beltane's, on the way to where they were going. Malcolm was just a little late in meeting up with Kate because of last minute details at the forge. When he arrived where Kate was waiting, he knew something was up. She wasn't smiling with her bright face as she normally did. She got down from her carriage, marched over to Malcolm, and said, "Where have you been? You've kept me waiting fifteen minutes at least, and I don't have time to wait around and just do nothing."

"Kate, it's not that big a deal. I had to finish up on something, and I rushed extra fast to make up for lost time. I'm really sorry." As she boarded Malcolm's carriage, she continued to berate him for several miles, going over and over the same argument again and again. Malcolm thought to himself that she was certainly showing a side of herself that he didn't know existed in her. He looked at her as she went through her tirade and just smiled, knowing that she would eventually run out of things to say concerning this "crisis." He looked at it as their first fight. As he thought, she finally came to the end of it and realized that she had overreacted to the whole thing. Her smile came back, and she apologized for carrying on the way she had. She took his hand and rubbed it gently as they rode down the country lane.She then leaned over and pulled his head to hers and gave him a gentle kiss on the side of his face. He loved it when she did this. She was still the most wonderful woman in the world to him. He held her hand and caressed her arm as they enjoyed the countryside. He would glance over at her and just smile at the beautiful creature next to him. How fortunate he was.

"I do apologize, Kate. It won't happen again. Promise."

"It's alright. I'm past it now. I'm taking you to a tavern down the pike that I think you'll love. It's got a nice atmosphere and the food is good."

As they rode, they talked about anything and everything that came to mind. They would compliment each other and say sweet things to one another the whole way there. They never ran out of things to say. In fact, they never had enough time to say everything that was on their minds.

Upon arriving at the tavern, Malcolm pulled his carriage up to a vacant spot nearby and in they went.

"You know, this tavern is run by an Italian. Don't know how he ended up here, but he's the only one in the region," Kate said. They were shown to a table near the back that was very spacious, maybe big enough for four people. The server told them of the food that they served as Kate and Malcolm decided.

"Well, what do you think so far?" Kate asked.

"Very nice; I like it. The food selection looks good too . . . and so do you, pretty lady."

Kate blushed a little as she looked deep into Malcolm's eyes before she stared down at the table. She loved the way he would say nice things about her and make her feel treasured. She wasn't used to that, and it came as a most welcome gesture. He made her feel loved and wanted, not taken for granted. She hardly ever received compliments, that is unless she was with Malcolm. He never seemed to run out of them. His vocabulary was full of nice descriptive words, and he expended them at will to her.

While eating the delicious food that had just been brought to them, Kate extended her foot over to Malcolm underneath the table. Malcolm thought this was precious— doing things like this in public, basically right in front of people that were none the wiser. They finished and opted not to take dessert. Kate insisted on paying the tab as she always did, especially since her successful investments would allow it, and they were on their way back to Forfar. The time again seemed too short. Malcolm always hated to end his time with Kate. They did manage to do a lot of talking on the way back, but their day together was about over. They had already chosen their next outing and were making their plans for that meeting. After Malcolm dropped Kate back at her carriage, they kissed each other passionately as two people in love would do and bid each other farewell. All the way home, Malcolm thought over every aspect of their date and played it over and over in his mind to relive the wonderful afternoon he had spent with Kate. He would now pretend to Ian that it was just another business appointment and go from there. Tomorrow was another day. Malcolm also thought about what it would be like to be married to Kate. In his mind it would be great. Could he adjust to a new and different woman in his life full-time? He thought he could. He figured that the good would outweigh any bad. Would she even consider marrying him? After all, she was engaged to someone else. How she could stay with her fiancé was beyond Malcolm. He didn't believe that there could be any real love between them. If anything, it was more of a convenience relationship. Malcolm knew that for her, too, it would be an adjustment, but so what? That's what life is sometimes. Things just don't always remain the same. All Malcolm knew was that he wanted her at his side every day. What would it take to accomplish that? How could he convince her to go with him and start over with the love they shared with one another? She did not want to change her lifestyle. It was almost like she loved her present circumstances more than anything else, or was afraid to venture out from what she would probably term her "safe place?" Unlike Malcolm, she had many women friends with whom she regularly associated, which was part of the lifestyle she relished. It didn't mean that all parts of her life would have to change. Malcolm wasn't a dictatorial type of person. He was actually easy to get along with. He knew he could make Kate happy, and that's all that mattered. Malcolm was ready for this change in his life, and he wanted Kate to be part of the change.

Fifteen

"Daniel, why do these Indians wear their hair in such a strange style? I've not seen hair shaved in such a manner before," Adam asked.

"Well, even though they are part of the Iroquois Nation, they have their own tribal ways. They are called Mohawks. They were not the first tribe though to wear this style. The Wyandot tribe was really the first to wear this haircut. I've seen some strange sights in the wilderness that I've traveled. Strange I suppose, by white man's standards, but normal by their own. All cultures are different, but we're all still human. It makes life more interesting," Daniel replied. "This country does indeed offer a variety of differences. It seems like the whole country is still up for grabs as the European countries vie for the right to claim land," Adam said.

"You know, your long white beard and robes make you stand out pretty well also, Adam. They may think that you're a strange fellow yourself."

"I suppose you are right, Daniel. I've not met anyone quite like myself except for my fellow Druids. You know, the Indians here remind me of our own Scottish roots with some of the Highlanders and early Picts back home. Some of them wore next to nothing, sometimes nothing at all, and painted themselves as well, just like these natives do."

"You know, it seems that you just can't get away from war or the eminence of war. Here we are, prisoners of the French. Who knows, are the British and French getting themselves ready to battle for this land of the colonies?" Daniel asked. "You would think with all the wars Britain has fought with their neighbors over there, that they could have come to some sort of understanding by now on how to get along. This country has great opportunity, but also a great climate for more war," Daniel continued.

"If it weren't for these mountains, I think they would have already been at each other's throats. This natural barrier has held them back at least this long," Adam responded.

"Yes, but here are the French, trespassing on British lands for the sake of some treasure when they know it is not their place. I wonder how many times the British have done the same thing. I think this is why there are so many battles—no one respects another's boundaries," Daniel said."You also have to consider the trespass on Indian lands. We have pushed them back many miles into the wilderness as we arrive by the boat-full to claim land that is not our own. We're moving in all along the eastern coast as fast as we can get here. I try at least to show respect for the Indians by trading with them on even terms as best I can. I seek not to cheat them or take advantage of them in my dealings. Whatever we bargain for from them should be of equal trade. I wonder how this great land will survive. What will become of it? Look at them— gathering up precious gems, taking from the earth without even thinking of repaying or thanking the earth for its bounty. It's like a bunch of buzzards feeding on a carcass. They can't get enough in their bellies. Now they're making the Indians think the same way. I've hunted these lands for awhile now, but have never witnessed this. I'm seeing a new side of my Iroquois brothers and it isn't pretty," Daniel said to Adam.

As Daniel and Adam contemplated their predicament, the French commander snapped out orders in his own tongue to his men. He seemed agitated and also in a hurry to finish up. His men had a look of fear on their faces because of the countenance of their leader. Apparently, he had a tyrannical attitude and demanded respect from hismen and abhorred slothfulness. The Frenchman motioned one of his subordinates over to him and whispered to him in private. After that,the footman came over to Daniel and Adam and requested that they follow him back to the commander. Daniel and Adam got to their feetand walked toward the French commander.

"We are about ready to depart this area of the country. We have overstayed our welcome, I perceive, and must be on our way. What to do with you and your robed friend? If I leave no witnesses, I will be safer. On the other hand, I am a man of loyalty. My country has no great friendship with the British, but we do with the Scottish. I know you are of Scotland, no?" the French commander asked.

"Aye, I am from Forfar on the east coast and Adam here is from that same area. Our countries have favored each other in many battles with the English as we continue to struggle for freedom from them," Daniel said.

"It is because of that alliance that you both will be set free . . . after you sail with us up the river for a day's distance. We must have that cushion so we may be sure of our rightful departure to our freedom. You do understand, Monsieur?"

"Seems we're in no position again to bargain," Daniel said. As camp broke up, the Frenchmen tore down their dwelling places and packed their bags as fast as they could. Canoes and other carved out boats were loaded almost to sinking. Arms were loaded and ammunition was stored aboard each canoe in case one sank and they lost all means of defending themselves. Many boats were already moving up river as others were preparing to take off as well. The commander stood watching all of this take place with his hands folded behind him rocking on his heels. His head swayed back and forth to get a good look at everything. Occasionally, he spoke in French to whomever was not performing his job right. He was a perfectionist. The Indians also hustled to complete their tasks and leave the area. The long-house they had built would be left behind for whoever would want to occupy it. They would erect new ones quickly when needed. It would be no secret to anyone coming upon these homes that it was the Iroquois who had built them since they had a recognizable style. They headed up the Connecticut River, back to French territory and safety. As Daniel and Adam were directed to one of the boats, the commander boarded another one with a few of his officers. Daniel and Adam were placed in the middle of the boat and made comfortable. Their sacks were placed in the floor of the boat near them. They had no weapons at this point, a safety precaution by the French. The group was a regular flotilla as they negotiated the river with at least twenty boats of various sizes and lengths. Some of the Indians were left on shore and walked or ran the path by the shore. Sure-footed and fast, they easily kept pace with the boats going upstream. The natives traveling on foot prepared the camp at the appointed place when all the canoes came ashore for the night.

The scenery was beautiful along the river and very quiet except for the splash of the paddles hitting the water. An abundance of birds called in the forest around them; it was like being in a bird sanctuary. Daniel could not identify many of the birds. Daniel noticed that Adam was content to just float along the river absorbing all the information he could gather. This was all so new to him— meeting strange people and traveling. Daniel also knew that Adam was looking forward to being back on his own again, away from the people who sapped his energy and stifled his creative life force. Adam knew that tomorrow he and Daniel would be free to run the woods once more. Daniel could almost make out a smile on the Druid's face, but not quite. Daniel was just glad he was Scottish.

Jack Bryson had already made a plan in his mind on how to apprehend Daniel MacGow. Jack was a very clever fellow and skilled woodsman himself. He could track a deer that had been dead for a week and find the carcass where it had fallen. He had tracked men on more than one continent. Forest and woodland areas were all the same to him. He was head and shoulders above regular woodsmen. He was a soldier and killer. He loved what he did and never grew tired or bored with his work. He lived only to complete a job and then looked for another one. He had been born to his work. He wasn't looking for retirement or an easy life of relaxation. His only aim was to please his boss, Theodore Higginbottom.

Tracing where Daniel MacGow was last seen was not a challenge. Jack Bryson knew Daniel was traveling with a partner, a strange fellow from Europe who was not familiar to Jack. Nevertheless, two would be easier to track than one. Jack knew that they had moved fast and without time to think; they would have made mistakes and left clues. They had left good footprints and plenty of broken twigs and branches. Jack felt like he was getting free money for this. Jack was cocky as well as mean and nasty. He had all the things that he would need to go on a forced march and stay out for weeks if necessary. He was armed with hidden knives and pistols, cords for strangling, and even metal rings to fit on his hands in case of a fist fight. He was prepared. If he ran out of food, he was a capable hunter or could eat from the plants he encountered or even go without food for longer than most. He had taken his horse a good part of the way before abandoning it to take up the chase on foot. After so many miles, he had come upon a small hunting party of about five or six Mohawks, but managed to stay out of sight until they had passed by. He was so close to them that he could hear their breathing from the exertion of their pace. They did not even know Jack was close enough and capable enough to have killed most of them before they knew what had happened.He saw no need to alert any more of them that might be in the vicinity.

Continuing to move through the woodland, Jack Bryson eventually came to the camp that Daniel and Adam had stayed in several nights ago. He found the fire pit and pine boughs that had served as their beds that night and many footprints in front of the camp that had been made by white men and maybe three or four sets by Indians. Who were these white men and Indians, he thought? This had him perplexed for the moment. He knew he would find out sooner or later. All the prints moved in the same direction: toward the west and the river. Some sort of war party maybe, but who were the white men?As Jack continued his tracking, he knew he was getting close to the river by the smell. He thought he heard it for a moment. Maybe not. Keeping his senses alert for danger, he finally came to the clearing and the long-house that had housed the Indians and the white men he had been tracking. Cautiously looking through the now empty structure, he knew they had left.

Something caught his eye though on the ground just ahead of him, a stone of unusual formation with sparkling facets. A gem of some kind. Odd, he thought, having such a stone right here on the ground in plain sight.

As he walked up to it and bent down to examine it further, there was a sudden whizzing sound, a thud, and then an arrow was sticking out of his left thigh. Feathers on the end of it showed it to be Mohawk. They had ambushed him and caught him by surprise. With no time to berate himself over his mistake, he quickly hobbled to safety at one end of the long-house and hid behind a wooden table that had been left behind. It had the residue of vegetables that had been prepared on it. He snapped the feather end of the arrow off and cursed it before throwing it across the hut in anger. The arrow had penetrated several inches into his leg, so it was necessary to push it the rest of the way through his leg and out the other side. He was bleeding profusely, but he was able to wrap a piece of cloth around it for the time being.Grabbing two of his pistols, he leveled them toward the clearing of the hut and waited for the second attack. His breathing was labored at this point with heavy heaves of his chest trying to replace the air that he had just expended. Every fiber of his being was on alert now as he thought about the hunting party that had passed him many hours ago. It had to be the same group, he thought.It had become deathly quiet at this point. Even the birds were silent. This was a sign that the hunters were still there, looking and waiting for him to make a mistake. Jack knew that he had to treat his wound properly soon or it would certainly get worse. He pulled out a flask of his favorite whiskey and poured some of it on his leg wound before taking a swig for himself. It burned his leg like a hot poker, but he knew it was necessary. He took another drink and put the flask away for now. He wanted to live to enjoy it later. Not the best position to be in, he thought to himself, but I've been in worse. If all they have are bows and arrows, or maybe tomahawks, I'll have the advantage with my pistols and musket.As he set his eyes to the wooded area beyond the clearing, he strained to see what others might not. He trained his vision to look beyond the first layer of what the brain says is there and bring into focus that which he was targeting. He had to shut out the obvious, and when he did, there it was, the target, well hidden, but now in sight. One of the braves was poised in a tree while two others were on the ground under the same tree. He aimed his musket, drew a bead, and squeezed the trigger. The powder flashed and a tremendous roar sounded as the charge hit its intended target and the Indian fell from the tree with an agonizing cry. The two on the ground scurried out of the way of the falling body to a new location.

Keeping his pistols handy, Jack began to reload and prepare for the next volley. Three arrows flew into the hut and hit on the overturned table while one flew over his head to the back of the hut. He wondered if he should wait for darkness or even out the odds first. He knew he had to vacate eventually.

As he finished reloading, he heard a thud on the roof of the hut. It wasn't heavy enough to have been a man . . . then he saw smoke and heard the crackling of fire. They had torched the hut, and were burning him out. His mind was made up for him—he had to leave.He gathered his things, limped to the back of the hut and crashed through to the outside near the dense forest. Getting back to his feet, he ran into the wooded area for a few hundred feet and paused by a tree. His breathing was once more at full capacity. Had they followed him? Had he lost them? Where were they?

Jack could hear the blaze in the distance and smell the smoke as well. Pretty hostile hosts, he mused to himself. Even though his life was at stake, he didn't lose his head to fear or make decisions that would put him in jeopardy. He was a logical man as well as a shrewd one. He still had his mind on his mission and saw this situation as a temporary delay.

Poking his head out quickly and then back again, he had a glimpse of one of the braves not too far away behind a tree that didn't completely hide him. As soon as he ducked back into safety, an arrow stuck in the tree he was behind. He hit upon a plan. Taking his pack off, he secured it to the front of his body and around his neck. Taking a pistol in each hand, cocked and loaded, he charged out from behind the tree toward where the Indians would be.

Just as he expected, two of them came into view on the path with complete confidence that they had the upper hand with bows bent and arrows fixed on Jack Bryson. In a split second, they loosed their arrows, right at the heart of Jack, but the pack intercepted the wooden shafts as they stuck in his rations within seconds of each other. The arrows did not penetrate. At the same time, Jack fired his two guns at close range and hit one brave in the forehead and the other in the stomach. Jack continued his run toward them, taking out his knife and finishing the wounded warrior.

Darting back into the woods, he took another path through the dense forest and continued his hobbled run. Twirling his backpack around his neck, he placed it back in its correct position and just in time as a single arrow found its mark in the pack to join the other two. They were not giving up, but neither was Jack.

Finding shelter behind a group of rocks, he turned to see how close his pursuers were. One was close enough to be on him in just a few seconds. He aimed his musket once more as the brave threw his hatchet, barely missing Jack as he fired the mighty gun again. The brave fell in a heap to the ground. Reload, reload, Jack thought to himself. Don't be caught with empty guns—too late: a brave threw himself on Jack with knife in hand. As the brave slashed wildly and cut him on the left arm, Jack flinched only slightly, taking hold of the Indian brave's arms to prevent him from using the knife any further. Jack was a strong man, having fought hand to hand in Europe many times and obviously winning. He got the brave turned over and managed to turn the knife to the brave's chest and thrust it deeply into him. A final breath escaped the brave warrior.

Was that five or six dead? Jack quickly reviewed the events and . . . one more, he concluded. Jack was exhausted and wounded. He did not want to go hand to hand again; he wanted this over now. He reloaded his pistols only and listened for any sound that might indicate where the final Indian was. Hearing rustling in the nearby trees, he turned to see the last Indian running away in the opposite direction, away from Jack. At least he would have time to mend his wounds now. Pulling out pieces of cloth from his pack, that was just what he did. The cut on his arm wasn't extremely deep, and the wound in his thigh would heal in time if he could keep the bleeding down. He was disappointed that this encounter would slow him down somewhat and that the last remaining Indian might go for reinforcements, but Jack was committed to finding Daniel and doing what he was hired to do. He would pull himself together and continue his mission.

As the day was ending, Daniel saw that the lead canoes were pulling onto shore. Several were already docked as the rest of them followed suit. Daniel and Adam were now poised to separate from the French and be on their way. Several braves, who had run the entire distance, were on shore. They too were a hearty bunch. Fires were already started and dinner was cooking even as they trod ashore. The canoes were secured and guarded by several braves so that nothing would be stolen or become unmoored. They had a lot of valuable treasure and supplies that they would need for their return home to French territory the next day.

Daniel and Adam collected their packs and supplies and were eager to be on their way. They were way off course from where they had started, and Daniel wanted to get on the road as soon as possible. Even with nightfall coming on, they preferred to be on their own.

"Monsieur, you are welcome to stay the night and enjoy our hospitality since the night is coming fast," said the French commander. "No, thank you, but we would prefer to say bon-jour and make camp on the way back to our lands. We thank you for honoring your word to allow us to leave peacefully and uninjured," Daniel remarked. "As you wish. May you have a peaceful journey to your lands and good luck to you both."

Picking up their packs, Daniel and Adam slung them over their backs and couldn't help noticing how heavy they felt. They had been mostly full, but still they felt heavier. Daniel tipped his cap to the commander with a salute, and off they went into the darkened forest to find their way to their own destination. As they occasionally glanced back, the fires glowed dimmer each time. They had a long way to go, farther for Adam since he had to travel almost all the way back to Salem while Daniel was still going to meet with the chief that he knew so well. At least the branch that he knew had not been as involved with the French so this episode would not be repeated. There were four of the branches of the Iroquois Nation that dealt heavily with the French. Daniel was just looking for a place to hide out with friends until he would be able to return to Salem. He was still a wanted man. "Up ahead is a place that looks good enough for our camp tonight," Adam said as he pointed to an area that had a rock face for a backdrop to protect their backs.

"That does look like our best hope for tonight, old friend. The rock face area it is then," Daniel confirmed.

They were both elated to be free and unscathed from their French captors and able to roam as free men once more. Daniel was beginning to understand more and more about what freedom meant from the harsh lessons he was learning in the American colonies. Freedom was still something that had to be earned and protected. There were always those who would try to take it from him and prevent him from achieving his goals. Vigilance was the never-ending price to pay.

Sitting around their fire after cooking a refreshing meal, Daniel and Adam were both thinking the same thing: "I hope we don't wake up with captors at our doorstep in the morning."

After making ready to turn in for the night, Adam was fixing his pack to double as a pillow when he felt something that just didn't feel right in the pack. Digging down through his belongings and supplies, he pulled out a few rocks, gemstones to be accurate.

Daniel, watching Adam rummage through his things, started doing the same thing, and to his amazement, he too had gemstones in his pack.

"Can you believe this? They actually paid us for our inconvenience while we were French captors," Daniel said. "There must be enough value here for a year's wages for this area."

"We'll certainly have a heavy pack to carry on our trip back," Adam said.

"My plan was to meet with the Iroquois chief on this side of the mountains and hopefully become his guest for a while, but now, with this small fortune, I may have to rethink my plans," Daniel said. "I have the means to travel anywhere in the colonies now and have the ability to take care of any expenses I might incur."

"That is all well and true, Daniel, but Higginbottom has the ability to ferret you out in civilization. With your Indian brothers, you will be afforded better protection."

"That's true enough, but I won't be able to do much fighting out here. I could possibly hire protection and devise a plan to upset his plans in Salem, maybe turn public opinion against him and put a stop to his satanical plans."

"Let's sleep on it tonight and think about it tomorrow," Adam said. As the first light shown through the canopy of trees, Adam was already up and had started breakfast when Daniel finally awoke to start the new day.

"I'll have a cup of that coffee if you haven't drank it all by now," Daniel said to Adam. Looking around the camp, he couldn't make out where Adam was. "Adam? Where are you this beautiful morning?" Daniel was feeling especially chipper now that they were no longer with the French and had a bright outlook starting this day off.

"If my Irish brothers were here they would say, 'Top o' the morning to ya.' Adam, are you still among the living?" Daniel lightheartedly said.

Walking a short distance from the camp, Daniel relieved himself and then looked all around the area, trying to get a fix on where Adam might be. He walked back into camp and poured himself a cup of hot coffee, sipping it to make it cooler to the tongue. Walking around the area, he tried to pick up a trail that Adam might have taken. It looked as though he had left from the east side of the camp, but the trail disappeared after just a few steps. Was Adam trying to hide his tracks or what?

Squatting down by the fire, Daniel took a few more sips of his coffee and wondered why Adam was not responding to his calls. It certainly wasn't like him to go away without saying a word. He wouldn't have left his backpack with everything he needed inside. Daniel sat down on a nearby log to ponder his next move. He began to notice how quiet the woods were this morning— not a good sign. That usually meant that something had scared the wildlife, and that was something to take notice of. Just to be on the safe side, Daniel went for his pistol, which lay by his pack.

"Just let it lie, MacGow," came a voice Daniel did not recognize. "Just take a seat back on the log you found so comfortable."As Daniel did as he was told, a man came walking into camp with two pistols aimed at Daniel.

"You're a hard man to catch up to, MacGow. The river diversion really threw me off somewhat, but I persuaded one of our Indian brothers to fill me in on the details before I slit his throat. He was most cooperative. By the way, since I know so much about you, allow me to introduce myself. I am Jack Bryson, of his Grace, Theodore Higginbottom. Name mean anything to you?" Jack asked.

"I know the scum. What have you done to my Druid friend, Adam?" Daniel asked.

"Believe it or not, he's fine. Well, not fine, but alive. I figure that with him alive, you'll be more likely to want to go back to Salem with me. When we're close enough, I'll set him free. I could arrest him also for helping an escaped fugitive from justice, but I'm not all bad. If you cooperate, I'll let him alone. Now you will be a good Scot and put these manacles on, right?"

Daniel complied and put the handcuffs on, locking them into place on his wrists. He had no choice, not with Adam's life in jeopardy. Otherwise, he would have at least put up a fight.

"I want to see Adam. Take me to him," Daniel demanded.Adam was not far away. He was tied to a tree with a gag in his mouth to keep him silent. When Daniel saw him, he was relieved. Adam was a little bruised, but in good condition. Jack cut him loose and marched them back into camp, Daniel in front with his cuffs on. "Pick up your things and we'll be on our way," Jack said.

Daniel had trouble getting his pack on with the handcuffs and with the extra load of gems in his pack. He was not going to tell Jack about his treasure even if he had to carry a heavy load while manacled.Adam was bound, but able to lift his pack into place. Jack had made sure they were both unarmed before the march began. Daniel had noticed that Jack was obviously limping and had very bad blood stains on his left leg. He also noticed that Jack seemed to stumble and weave somewhat as they walked. After a few miles on the trail, Jack suddenly went down on one leg.

"Hold it right there. I have to make a pack adjustment here," Jacksaid.

Adam also now took notice of Jack's increasing weakness. Adam had regained his composure and some strength and was looking for an opening to get control of the situation once again.

"Take a five minute break. You both look tired," Jack said.They both watched Jack while he grimaced in pain and put pressure on his leg. His face was red, and perspiration was dripping from his nose and down his face. Daniel concluded that Jack must be getting sicker from the wounds. If they waited a little while longer, the wound would help them make their escape.

"Daniel, over here," Jack commanded.

He directed Daniel to a tree and tied him there securely.

"You, over here on the other side of the tree," Jack told Adam.When Jack had them both secured to the tree, he lay down about ten feet from them with his musket aimed toward them and drifted in and out of consciousness. Jack mumbled something incoherent as his fever rose.

"I don't know what you did to Mr. Higginbottom, but you're going to pay, mister, you're going . . . to pay . . . you're going . . . you're . . . going to . . ."

Jack's musket fell loose from his fingers and slowly tumbled down to the ground beside him. Jack was unconscious and defenseless.

"Adam, see if you can pull loose from your ropes. Can you reach my knot to untie it?" Daniel asked Adam.

"I believe I can. It looks like he was too weak to do a good job on knot tying today. There's a lot of slack in the rope, and it's beginning to strain a little. A bit of applied friction and . . . there, it's broken through. Give me just a minute, Daniel, and I'll have us both out of here."

After finally freeing himself and Daniel, Adam made sure that Jack was truly out cold, and they gathered their belongings. They disarmed Jack completely and took his boots off for good measure. They didn't have any feelings that were good toward him and left him there to fend for himself. They hit the trail and took no time to look back. They were going to put distance between themselves and Jack.

"Have you thought about where you might go, Daniel?" Adam asked.

"I was thinking about going further south, maybe into Virginia or North Carolina. There's plenty of land to hunt down there with game like you wouldn't believe. Of course, I'd have to make friends with the Powhatan and the Tuscarora, but I'm easy to get along with, don't you think, Adam?"

"I have unfinished business in Salem and will wait for your return one day. Higginbottom's kind can't last forever, so I'm sure we'll meet again soon," Adam said.

"Then it's good-bye for now, old friend, and I'll see you, hopefully by Samhain," Daniel replied.

Sixteen

As night fell, the participants were filing in to the back room of the MacGregor house for their monthly full moon meeting of the Enlightened Ones. The wealthy, powerful, and influential controlled everything they could while looking and sounding like everyday regular people. Secretly though, they were a sect of an even bigger group who were out for world domination. They believed they had been chosen to bring in a new order of rule to mankind.

Giving their secret signs to the Master of Ceremony, they were admitted as they showed their ring hand to him and he nodded. The lightning bolt insignia was the identification sign for this sect. Other groups elsewhere had their own sign for their people in their part of the world.

As the leader called the meeting to order, introductions were made and the agenda was read to the members present. A presenter told of events that they had been a part of this past month and any successes or failures that they had. As each spoke of his own participation in community affairs, a certain Mr. Alexander Taggart, the constable from the Tolbooth, told of his monthly experience.

"I have kept abreast of events involving Mr. Malcolm MacGow and his investigation into the dead Druid and what the magistrate talked about with him. They are aware of the triangle and the properties involved. I don't believe they have pieced it together as yet," Mr. Taggart said.

"Are they suspicious of you and your role in this?" spoke the leader.

"Not to my knowledge. I am but another constable going about his duty to them."

"Keep up the good work and you will be elevated to a higher level within the brotherhood very soon," said the leader. "You are next, Mr. Howard. What have you to report?"

"After attending a special meeting within the church, I've learned that there are a few parishioners who are dedicated to helping Mr. MacGow. I was invited to their ridiculous Christian gathering since they think I'm one of them," Kevin Howard said.

"You are doing a great job there, Mr. Howard. We would have you stay at that post, as tough as it is."

As others spoke about the parts they played in their community, the leader seemed pleased with their results. However, he still had concern about acquiring the MacGow property. The MacGows were stubborn people and had support from others in the community, which greatly annoyed the leader. He knew he had to find the answer to getting his hands on that piece of property. After all had completed telling the group of their monthly activities, the leader made a request. "Let us call upon the Watchers, the Mighty Ones, to enrich our endeavors and bring victory to our cause. Let us pay homage to ONE ABOUT WHOM NAUGHT MAY BE SAID," spoke the leader. After much prayer, the group concluded other business. Then the leader spoke of the interference of the Druids. Over the centuries, there had been many battles with them, and they had become one of their arch rivals. They had, as Enlightened Ones, fought them in Rome over sixteen hundred years ago when Christianity was starting to become an acceptable religion to the Roman state. The weavers of magic and spells were cast out, and with them, the Druids. They were all merged together by Roman law, and so had begun a never-ending quest to eradicate them wherever they were found. This brought the present circumstances into proper context. The battle still raged. "We will one day rule this planet. That is our destiny. We are the fortunate ones who have been selected to protect our Masters' secrets from interlopers and intruders who stand in the way of the attainment of the objectives of the Enlightened Ones," spoke the leader.

"We will continue to discuss plans to evict the MacGows from our land and formulate a plan to fulfill our goals in this area. We will not disappoint our master," the leader continued.

This group of men had sold their souls to this evil cause and had aligned themselves with men who had no conscience when it came to fulfilling their goals and wayward plans. This was the same group who, in the early 1660's, had developed the heinous plan of witch accusations. The same group, now in the Americas, led by Theodore Higginbottom, were doing the same thing to colonists. It was an old idea to use against a new group of people for Higginbottom's bidding: convincing the masses in the church that there were, indeed, witches in their midst and at the same time, making Mr. Higginbottom the hero and savior of the colonists. It was, as the Latin saying goes, Ordo Ab Chao—order out of chaos.

As their meeting went on through the night, they were not the only ones out and about. Louis Mar and a few Druids were watching the activities of this group. They had stationed themselves in various places throughout the farm to watch and listen for anything they could glean from this despicable mob. The Druids were forever vigilant in their age-old feud with the Enlightened Ones. They knew that this group used unscrupulous and illegal means that were hurtful to innocent people. They knew that the EnlightenedOnes looked at others as mere cattle and not even as human beings and that they would not let feelings or morality stand in their way to rebuild the earth in their image, even if their actions destroyed it. These people were more evil than the invented witches they preached about. They, for the most part, persecuted women, and a few men also. They sought to undo what God had done— destroy the world order and make ready for the new.

"Keep your eyes and ears open, my brothers, for we fight against them who hate us and everyone not aligned with them," Louis said."Why don't we just rush them and kill them all now?" spoke the Druid next to Louis Mar.

"Because they are still more than we are. Also, do you not know the code we live by? We are not murderers, but strike only in defense of ourselves or others.No, we will observe and be patient and wait for the time to strike when all is in correct alignment. They cannot get to Malcolm, for we are ever on guard for him. Our biggest problem is combating the misuse of authority in this land as they contrive ways to make it work for them. Besides, they have guards posted, as you can see, and they might be able to alert the others inside. Don't let your impetuousness get you in trouble," Louis said.

The other Druid heeded the words of his mentor and thought about the problem that might result from his actions. He had learned a valuable lesson tonight.

In the wee hours of the morning, the Enlightened Ones broke up their meeting. They filed out, one right after another, and didn't stop to socialize as they unhitched their horses and carriages. They made their way down the long road of the farm and onto the main road as they went to their homes and went about their business. The last one out blew out the last candle, and the house fell completely dark.The Druids kept their places as they watched everything unfold before their eyes. They kept a mental picture of the ones who had attended the meeting so they would have some idea about who was scheming their terrible plots. Louis had the idea of going back into the house when everyone was gone to uncover whatever evidence he could find. As the last member left the farm and headed down the road, Louis dismissed his fellow Druids and proceeded to enter the house from a side door that he easily opened by merely picking the lock. The previous renter, Mr. MacGregor, had lived sparsely, but apparently that was all he had needed. The front rooms were cluttered with old furniture and odds and ends with a big fireplace and mantle. Several pokers were leaning up against the stone wall of the fireplace with a bucket and several logs for the next fire. There was a small bellows hanging from a hook with several loglifting devices. Louis cautiously made his way to the back of the house until he came to a door that wasshut with a latch and lock. He knew that had to be the room used for their meetings. It was the only locked room he had observed. Louis carefully picked the mechanism, and it suddenly clicked open. Upon entering the room, he lit a small candle and noticed that it was the cleanest room in the house with polished furniture and nice chairs scattered around the room. On the desk were several different pieces of paper and various holders containing more paperwork. Making himself comfortable in the chair behind the desk, he began to read the collection of information before him. "TO REGIONAL DIRECTOR, STRATHMORE DISTRICT: IT HAS COME TO OUR ATTENTION THAT YOU ARE NOT MAKING THE PROGRESS YOU PROMISED AT OUR LAST DISTRICT MEETING. WE NEED TO ACQUIRE THE PROPERTY IN QUESTION AS SOON AS POSSIBLE SO THAT OUR OTHER PLANS MAY PROCEED. WE ARE COUNTING ON YOU AS A TRUSTED OFFICER OF ORGANIZATION.THE DIVINE ONE."

As Louis continued to read other materials, he came across other local citizens who were marked for "special treatment and observation" within the community, citizens who might be a stumbling block to the Enlightened Ones plans or even ones who could be recruited. Louis found it hard to believe that they would go this far in their pursuit of their deadly goals of wanting to affect the whole of the town and all in it.

As Louis continued to riffle through the papers, he heard a door shut somewhere in the house. He knew someone else was now in here with him. Blowing out the candle, he moved to the door to exit, but heard the sound of someone walking near the entranceway to the room he was now in. Louis moved quickly behind the door and pulled his hood over his head and waited. Moments later, someone arrived at the door.

"I could have sworn I locked this door when I left. I must be getting old," said the man who had led the meeting.

As the man moved to the desk to retrieve his paperwork, Louis silently moved out of the room and down the hallway, finding the side entrance, stepping like a cat after its prey. In a moment, he was gone into the woods and back to his camp with the other Druids.

Malcolm was up early and preparing his favorite riding horse for the pupils who would learn to ride today. Ian was going to fire up the forge and carry on that part of the business, which worked out quite well for both of them. As Malcolm was saddling up the horse, two ladies arrived, one for riding lessons and the other just for moral support.

"Good morning, ladies. Ready for your lesson this bright and crisp morning?" Malcolm asked.

"Yes sir. I'm a little sore though from last time so go easy on me," said the trainee.

"We'll give you an extra blanket to sit on so the horse won't bounce you so much until you can toughen up a bit," Malcolm said. The lessons were going well as the pupil adjusted to the slow gallop of her horse, and her friend watched from the split rail fence with excitement on her face. The road in front of Malcolm's forge was getting quite busy already as some would stop to watch how his pupils were progressing.

"Pay them no mind; they are merely curious, but you must concentrate on the business at hand. Keep control of the horse; don't let him lead you, but rather you show him which way you want to move. You are the boss when you sit upon the beast. Use your hands on the reins and your feet and legs to direct him. Let him know who's the master. That's a girl. Keep him moving . . . now stop. Make him stay where you want to stop."

Malcolm's pupil was learning a lot this day. He knew she was gaining more confidence with each session. Her friend looked pleased, but was too shy and not up to trying it herself. As Malcolm schooled his pupil in equestrian exercises, Ian came out from the forge to ask assistance of Malcolm.

"Dad, I need your help in straightening out a piece of metal for a pike I'm making for Mr. MacKeller."

"Okay, son. Be right there."

Malcolm excused himself from the lesson and attended to Ian and the forge problem. "That's quite a piece of metal you've got there, Ian. Is it going to be strong enough?" he asked.

"Oh, yes. I've tested it several times now, and I'm positive it'll hold. The grip is formed just the way MacKeller asked, because he's got enormous hands and wanted it a little bigger for his size." "Okay, just as long as you're sure. Of course, no one else will be able to use it, but why would he unless he was killed," Malcolm said."Thanks for the hand; I think I'll be able to manage from here. Hey, looks like your next client is here. Isn't that Kate?"

Malcolm took a look out to the yard and recognized that it was Kate. He noticed how pretty she looked, and instantly his heart started beating in an unnatural rhythm. This was the way she always affected him. She made his heart flutter every time he was near her. She was the most perfect creature God had made. How thankful he was to have her in his life. He could think of no other and desired no other.He could truthfully say this, not only to her, but to himself. He knew in his heart that she was the one, the only one he would ever want again, and he made that perfectly clear to her every time they were together. Oh, how he loved her and desired her. He could never envision wanting another as she erased the memory of every woman he had ever known. His only regret was that he had not met her sooner in his life. She had been near his own hometown for many years, but he had never run across her in any casual or business occasion. Why was that, he wondered? Maybe it was just fate or an odd series of circumstances. He watched her from the forge and was mesmerized by her. He snapped back to the present and answered Ian.

"Yes, son, you're right. She's right on time. If you don't need me anymore, I'll head back out to the riders, but don't hesitate to call me if you want me for anything."

Finishing up with the current rider, he thanked her for coming and bid her good day. He had been looking at Kate while saying good-bye to the previous client and hoped she hadn't noticed his rude manners. "Kate, it's good to see you again."

He leaned close to her so that no one else would hear and said, "I love you!"

"I love you too!"

"I've got your horse here, if you're ready. You feeling okay?" "Yes, I'm doing alright."

After working in the yard with her riding lessons, they were coming to the end of their session. It was nearing noon and they had plans to go to the nearby town for a play that was performing there. The troupe was a traveling band of performers doing a pirate play for whoever would show up to watch. Kate knew they were in the area and wanted Malcolm to see them with her. They had agreed to meet at Roger's, a local market, on the way. It sold food and drink items to the people in the area and had been in business for a long time. As time drew near, Malcolm arrived first and then Kate not too long after that. She pulled her carriage into the area where she would leave it while they were away. Greeting each other was becoming a tradition with them. They loved to greet and fall into each other's arms.

Quickly they were on their way and headed to the theater for the play. The play had been there for awhile, and they were giving an afternoon performance. Arriving at the theater with time to spare, they decided to get something to eat first after the long trip on the road. Near the theater was a food establishment that featured many different varieties of foods to choose from. It was set up to accommodate the many travelers in this shopping bazaar. After selecting their food, they settled down to a table nearby to have an enjoyable lunch before the play. As they ate, they talked and looked into each other's eyes and thought about how fortunate they were to have each other.

"I think it's getting near time to go if we're going to make the show. If we walk fast, we'll make it," Malcolm said.

Arriving at the ticket window, Kate pulled her purse open and paid the girl at the window for two seats. Malcolm and Kate were shown to their seats on the end row off of the first aisle. They sat near the wall on the second row from the floor on a raised platform. They cuddled together, holding hands and giving each other gentle kisses on the lips. Surprisingly, there were not that many other people at the showing and they sat near the top of the aisle, which gave Malcolm and Kate more privacy and freedom of movement. As the show began, the candles were extinguished, and they sat back, still arm in arm, as close as they could get to one another. The show was a production about a pirate and his predicaments. Unfortunately, or fortunately, for Malcolm and Kate, they didn't get to really concentrate on the show as they became a bit naughty with their roving hands throughout most of the production. They were clever enough to disguise their actions and no one was the wiser, but they just did not care if they remembered the scenes in the play or not. Their attention to each other was far more important than anything happening on stage.

After the production was over, they calmly gathered their things and exited the theater, looking to shop some more before they went home.

"I can't believe we did that in there! I hardly saw any of the production, thanks to you," Kate jovially said.

"I'm sorry if I preoccupied your time in there, but I think ourproduction was better than theirs anyway," Malcolm said, unable to hold back a laugh.

They walked hand in hand in the market area, Kate looking for something to buy. She settled at a perfume counter and tried several different scents, even letting Malcolm sniff a few before deciding on a purchase that they both liked. She paid the vendor, and they were once again on their way back to the carriage and home to Forfar.

As they rode back to pick up Kate's carriage, she lovingly kissed Malcolm on the side of his face and then, causing his heart to flutter even more, she kissed his ears and caused chills to travel up his spine. She laughed when she did this because she too knew how that felt. Arriving back at the starting point at Roger's, they said their good-byes again and made each other late as usual. Malcolm watched her drive off and followed for a short distance before he turned off for his home. Malcolm knew he was most fortunate to have Kate. Having her in his life had changed him for the better, that he knew. "Kate, I love you, m'lady," Malcolm said to himself as he rode down the road. "I love you."

Seventeen

The journey south into Connecticut was a welcome relief for Daniel in that he had no known enemies there and hoped to not make any. Adam had headed back toward the Salem area and would have to go into hiding because of Jack Bryson. Adam hoped that Jack would not make it back since Jack could identify him and would not be lenient toward him if he was caught. Adam was good at hiding though, especially with his Druid brothers to protect him.

Daniel felt at home in the wilderness. He had hunted and trapped here and it was God's good grace that He allowed Daniel the freedom to wander these woods. He knew that he would encounter the Indians of the land eventually, but was not too concerned since he came in peace and took only what he needed to survive. He actually got along better with them than with some white men. Daniel continued to follow the Connecticut River south until he came near Springfield. He decided to skirt the perimeter of the town just in case Higginbottom had forewarned them about him. He was just being cautious and was leaving nothing to chance. He headed at an easterly direction toward the mountains, which he felt might provide him more protection. He had encountered no one else so far ever since he left Adam, not even an Indian hunting party or white hunters. Although Daniel had never been in this part of the country before, his backwoods skills enabled him to adapt quite well. He had seen a few deer and even some turkey in the short time he had been traveling through these woods. The forest was alive with many different species of birds, including eagles and hawks. He had fished for awhile back up the river just to see what might be found in these waters. The fishing was good. At least he knew he wouldn't starve.

Moving ever so near the mountain range made his heart leap. He always loved going high up in the hills to be able to look down on the valley below. It gave him a sense of the enormity of the area he traversed. He also noted that there were different varieties of wildlife at different elevations. The plant life was different, but he could figure out what or what not to eat. It was all beautiful though, and he felt at home, even in a strange wooded area.

Just this side of the mountain range, he noticed a clearing that looked like a small plot of land that had been plowed. He wondered who could be this far in the wilderness. He looked closer and confirmed that someone was living there when he saw a steady rise of smoke from a chimney. As he got closer, he could see the telltale signs of civilization in the ruts that had become a path to the field and various other scraps of trash. By the familiar animal scents, he knew there were a few cows and horses nearby. Several chickens cackled and ran as if they were being chased. Yes, someone lived here, that was for sure.

As he rounded the small hill which led up to the cabin, he heard the sound of raucous laughter that reminded him of some of the saloons he had been in before. There couldn't be a saloon way out here. What was it then? When the cabin came into view, his question was answered. Two white men and an Indian in white man's clothes, probably a half-breed, were giving the lady of the house a harder time than would be permitted in any civilized man's eyes. They had strewn her laundry all over the yard and were manhandling her in a most ungentlemanly fashion. One had a bottle of whiskey from which he freely chugged, while the other two maintained control of the woman. Her blouse was torn from one shoulder and the sleeve dangled down her side. Her hair was now hanging down from the pins that would normally hold it in position on top of her head. She looked like she had been thrown down more than once.

"Is that the way your mother taught you to behave in public, especially with a woman?" Daniel asked, pointing his musket at the group.

Surprised by the sudden appearance of Daniel, one of the men holding the woman let go long enough to pull his pistol from his belt and began to aim it at Daniel. Daniel, with no time to ask any more questions, fired his musket at him and hit him dead center in the chest, knocking him several feet back and into a woodpile, scattering the logs. The girl, in the meantime, had wrenched her arm free from the half-breed and threw herself away from the action of the fighting men. The half-breed, seeing that he had lost control of the girl, went for his musket, which was leaning against the fence. Dropping to one knee,

Daniel threw his musket down, pulled his own pistols from his belt, and fired at the half-breed, hitting him in the shoulder causing him to fall to the ground in great agony. The whiskey-drinking man fumbled for his own pistol, but was unable to get it loose from his belt. Daniel ran over to him and clubbed him with the pistol he held, knocking him unconscious.

Daniel rushed over to the woman to help her to her feet. "Are you all right, ma'am? Did they hurt you?"

"I think I'm okay. They bruised me somewhat, but I'm okay, thanks to you."

"Do you know these men? What did they want?"

"No, I don't know them. They said they wanted to have a little fun and offered me a drink, which I refused," said the woman, pulling hertorn sleeve back into place as best she could. "I've never had such ill treatment from anyone before, not even from the local Indian population. I guess that shows what too much drink will do to a man." Daniel tried getting the drunk man to his feet and also getting the wounded one to help his friend. The drunk was a little more sober now that he realized that he could have been killed. The other was holding his arm to stop the bleeding, from what was basically a flesh wound.

"Get your dead friend and move out of here. I don't ever want to see you on my property again," Daniel said, lying to present a threat if they ever came back.

Daniel made sure their guns were unloaded and snatched the sack hanging from the drunk's belt. Pulling out just enough coins to pay for the damage they had done, Daniel tossed the bag back to the drunk man and pointed the way out from the property. As they hauled their dead friend out of the woodpile, they struggled to move him, but finally made their way back down the trail that led out into the wilderness.

The yard was a mess—clothes that had been hanging from lines, were thrown everywhere and woodpiles torn down.The woman, with hands on hips, looked around the yard deciding where to start first. She was flustered and exhausted as she began picking up her laundry and hanging it on a line.

"Here, let me give you a hand. Why don't you get yourself a drink of water and sit over in the shade for a spell? I'll pick up your yard for you," Daniel said.

"Maybe I will; I'm not feeling too well right now. Thank you very much. By the way, my name is Logan Moss. I'm the owner of this house and property and have been for the past four years."

"I'm so happy to make your acquaintance. I'm Daniel MacGow from . . . up north." Daniel hesitated to tell her where he was from for fear of being discovered.

"I'm so glad you came along when you did, Mr. MacGow. I don't know what would have happened to me without your timely intervention."

"Call me Daniel. I'm just traveling south, doing some hunting and spending some time alone. I've never been in this part of the country, and I'm finding it most beautiful."

"I'm glad you like it, Daniel. I've been here for quite a while now. It's just me and my two children, Hamish and Rhiannon. They're in the house hiding since those brutes came by. And by the way, you can call me Logan."

"There's no Mr. Moss, if I could be so bold?" Daniel asked. "No, we parted company four years ago and we're on our own now. We manage quite well though, and we're happy out here away from the city life. Just the three of us in our little cabin is all we need right now."

Daniel sensed that she wasn't telling the complete truth by the way she hesitated in her speech. He just wasn't convinced by her tone. He figured she was glad to be apart from her husband for whatever reason that might be. She was managing as things were, but it was trying at times. She was a strong woman and capable of dealing with most situations that would arise. In a way, he envied her. She was on her own with no one else to answer to. She could come and go as she pleased. She was making it on her own. This was hard enough for a woman by herself, but she was raising two children and fending for herself. Daniel admired her.

After helping her pick things up from the yard and getting the woodpile back to a manageable stack, Daniel prepared to continue his walk up into the mountains. He had wasted enough time fighting with the riff-raff that had invaded Logan's property, and now it was time to make up lost ground before nightfall settled in.

"Well, if you don't need anything else, I'll be moving on. I want to make camp before nightfall."

"I'd like to repay you if I could. I'm deeply grateful for what you did today," Logan said.

"No payment needed, Logan. Anyone would have done the same thing."

"I don't think you'll make it up that mountain before nightfall. Why don't you stay for supper and bunk in the shed tonight and start fresh tomorrow? I make a mean rabbit stew, as the kids will attest to, with rolls and coffee you can't beat."

Daniel thought about how dark it was beginning to get, and rabbit stew sure sounded good to him right now. He hadn't seen or talked to anyone for awhile and the company would be good, at least for a night. "Okay, it's a deal.

But let me at least bring in the wood for the fire.'"Stew it is then. Grab your pack and come on in."

As Daniel approached the cabin, he could see the heads of the two children peering out from behind the door as he came near. Logan led the way, limping a little as she went. The cabin was small, but still roomy enough to accommodate her family. It was a typical cabin with no wasted space inside. She had hung utensils on the walls and everything else that could be hung. Daniel noticed she had a musket of her own in the corner and she looked quite capable of using it. She must have been taken by surprise by the three men when she was hanging the laundry. Otherwise, she would have blasted them back into the woods. Her children were staring at Daniel since he was a stranger, possibly afraid he might turn out to be like the other three bad men a few minutes ago. They were leery, which under the circumstances, was normal.

"Hey, kids, I'm Daniel MacGow," He held out his hand to welcome a shake. "You must be Hamish and Rhiannon."

The children did not respond but held a steady gaze at Daniel as he knelt down to be on eye level with them. "I hear your mother makes a great rabbit stew, and I can't wait to taste it."

"Our mom makes the best rabbit stew in the country," Hamish said, finally breaking the silence.

"That's right. She's the best!" Rhiannon added.

"Well I wouldn't go that far, Hamish. I may be the best in the mountains though," Logan agreed.

"I'll put it to the test. I'll let you all know after I'm done. Can I do anything to help, Logan?" Daniel asked.

"No, I don't think so. The children usually set the table and . . . you did wash your hands first, Hamish?" Logan asked.

"Well . . . I forgot, sorry," Hamish confessed.

"It's okay, Mom, I'll set the table," Rhiannon said.

"I guess I'd better join you, Hamish. I didn't wash mine either," Daniel laughed.

After everyone was ready to sit down to eat, Daniel was guided to the place at the table that would be considered the head. Everything was nice, and Logan poured the drinks for each of them. It was milk for the kids and coffee for Daniel and Logan.

"Daniel, we always say grace before eating, if you don't mind," Logan said.

"I do too, when I remember."

"Lord, we thank you for this bounty and for your love toward us and for Mr. MacGow, whom you sent this day to intervene on our behalf. Amen,"

Logan concluded.

"Mmm, this really is great stew. I don't believe I've ever tasted anything as good. My compliments to the chef, madam," Daniel complimented.

"We told ya. It's the best in the country," Hamish said.

"It's the best in the mountains," Rhiannon said.

"You know, I think it is the best in the whole country," Daniel agreed.

"Alright everyone, just eat it before it gets cold," Logan said with a big smile on her face.

"You know, I once knew a family of Moss back in Scotland. They used to live not far from us. They came up from the border country, I believe," Daniel said.

"My family is from the border country, but I never visited outside of my home area. I married my husband, who was from Aberdeen, and we settled in Killin, just north of Stirling, before moving to the colonies. Things were rocky from the start. My parents never really liked his attitude, and they knew he wasn't quite right for me. They proved to be right. He would always want to put me in my place and let me know that he was in charge. It was very hard living with him. I always felt like I was being watched. He just didn't make me feel loved. Well, to make a long story short, he eventually became violent with me on many occasions and had me terrified to even be around him. The children were also afraid of him, especially when he drank too much.

One night, in a tavern, he got into a fight with a man who was basically minding his own business and killed him. They sent him off to jail with no real prospect of getting out anytime soon. We moved in with a family in our area who happened to be moving to this part of the country, and so we joined them and came to this place. They live about three miles south of here and I see them ever so often. They even help me plow the fields in the spring for which I'm most grateful."

"I didn't mean to pry, but I was curious. Thank you for being forthcoming with me," Daniel humbly said.

"And what about you, Mr. MacGow? Married?"

"No, not me.Never been. I just hunt and trap and enjoy God's blessings each day. I came to the colonies to make my fortune and was doing fine until one day... you don't want to know about all that. Let's just say that life has led me this far, and I'm continuing the journey."

"Okay, let's finish up supper. Who's turn to do the dishes?" Logan asked.

"It's mine," Rhiannon said, dragging her voice as if she just didn't want to do them.

"Hamish, why don't you dry for her and that way she'll finish faster so you can both do your schoolwork I gave you," Logan suggested. He moped over to the basin with the dirty dishes and did it, but not enthusiastically. Overall, they were good kids who didn't get into too much trouble.

"Daniel, let me show you the shed where you're spending the night. I'm sure you won't find it too uncomfortable. There's plenty of room to unroll your bedroll and the roof doesn't leak," Logan said. "Okay, fine. By the way, that really was a good meal. It's been awhile since I ate home-cooked food," Daniel said, patting his stomach.

"While the kids are getting ready to study, would you like a glass of Scotch? I try to keep a bottle for medicinal purposes and celebrations. This seems like good enough reason to break it out," Logan delightfully said. She brought out two small glasses and poured a shot into each one, handing one to Daniel.

"By the looks of this bottle, you celebrate every chance you get," Daniel laughingly said.

"No, it's just that I've had this bottle for a long time because I don't know when I'll ever get another way over here in the colonies, so I drink it sparingly."

Daniel and Logan sat on the porch after setting up the shed for Daniel to stay in. She had constructed a porch swing big enough for two people which the children played too rough with most of the time, but it still held up pretty well. As they passed the time swinging gently and sipping their whisky, frogs, insects, and wildcats made the night seem like anything but a tranquil place to be. They both seemed to smile and laugh a lot as their conversation went from serious talk to light-hearted amusement. Logan's stories were as entertaining as Daniel's and they kept each other's attention as the night went on. "Are you sure all these things happened to you, or are they something you read?" Daniel asked in a teasing way.

"Are you calling me a liar, sir?" Logan giddily asked.

"No, m'lady, just not sure that one person could accomplish all those deeds by herself."

"I could take you to the exact spot and show you right where I shot that bear, and you can still see the bloodstains on the tree where I killed him." Logan grabbed the hand of Daniel to take him there. Daniel held her hand with his as he told her it was too late tonight. "I don't think we would be able to see bloodstains in the dark unless we turned into owls."

She paused for a moment and neither said anything, but they slowly ceased laughing and talking as they held each other in a steady gaze. Their faces slowly moved closer as they continued to hold hands and their lips found each other, and a soft kiss ensued, which they held for a few seconds. As they broke away, they looked at each other, still only inches apart and once again kissed, holding this one even longer. "I'm sorry, Logan. . . I had no right to do that. I've caught you at a vulnerable time and I took advantage. Forgive me."

"You've no need to apologize. I wanted to kiss you just as much. It felt . . . good and a welcome feeling that I thought I might have forgotten."

They held each other tightly while the swing easily swayed back and forth, sounding a noisy creak each time it moved. As they looked at each other, Logan rubbed her fingers down the face of Daniel and stroked his beard as he looked deep into her eyes. A few hours ago, he didn't even know this woman, now. . . well, he knew her better than any woman since he had come to the colonies. He had kept company and had get-togethers with young ladies before, but there was never any emotional attachment. With Logan, he felt something that had never hit him before. She was different in more ways than one. He had never had time for emotional things in his life; he was a hunter and that took up all his extra time. He was building his fortune and concentrated on that. This hit him like Higginbottom's men—flat in the face with no apologies.

He broke from Logan and said good-night to her. He was afraid, afraid of something he wasn't used to dealing with. He didn't know how to respond to his own emotions. He was embarrassed and afraid, all at the same time.

As Daniel made his way to the shed where he would spend the night, Logan looked dumbfounded and wondered if she had been too aggressive or had insulted Daniel in some way. She sensed his awkwardness as he left and didn't know what to say or do. She decided to get the children ready for bed and get a good night's rest herself. After all, she had been through a trying day.

Daniel lay on his back, watching the moon through the one small window of the shed. The beams hit him right in the face and nearly blinded him with their brilliance. He could not sleep anyway. He now had new thoughts to ponder and was trying to figure out what to do tomorrow. Was he leaving, going to the mountains like he had planned, or was he now somehow committed to Logan because of what had taken place on the porch tonight? He thought to himself that he would rather fight hostiles or some raging storm in the mountains than feel like he did now. Those things he could deal with, but this. . . he hadn't a clue.

Logan was also sleepless. She had not been with a man since her divorce. She had had the opportunity to go out a few times, but found men not to her liking. She stayed busy with the children and the never-ending chores that had to be done each day. Daniel had come out of nowhere, but was now slowly creeping into her heart. She was not a person of impulse, but she did feel comfortable with Daniel, like she had known him all her life. What was she to do with her feelings?"Why do I have feelings for this stranger," she asked herself. "Maybe it was too much rabbit stew," she thought. "I'm going to hate to see him go," she whispered to herself. "I'm happy here, just the three of us. We keep busy and the children are content. It has to be divine timing," she thought. "What with the mashers who attacked me and Daniel saving me, he had to be Heaven-sent."

They both drifted off to sleep at the same time, Daniel in his shed and Logan in her bunk. They awoke with the chickens asking for breakfast and the dog barking for the same. Daniel, flinging the covers off and folding his bedroll, threw open the door to let some light in. The dog came up to the shed and looked inside to see if the occupant was going to come out or not.

"Hey, pooch! Another day, huh, doggy?" Daniel said. Stretching his arms over his head, he heard the cabin door open as Hamish came out with a bucket to fetch some water from the nearby creek for breakfast and to wash up a bit.

"Morning, Hamish. Sleep well?"

"Yes, sir, I sure did, like a log."

"Your mother up yet?"

"I'm up, Daniel. First time though in a long while that the chickens got up before I did. I really needed that sleep," Logan said."You look great today, Logan. That sleep did wonders for you, not that you needed it to look great," Daniel said.

After breakfast, Daniel was putting his pack together for his trip up the mountain, looking over at Logan as he did so. She was staring at him, not saying a word but with a look on her face that he hadn't seen before from her. She was not smiling nor did she have a bright countenance as she twirled a piece of tall grass between her fingers. She sat on the step of the porch and just stared. Daniel knew what was going through her mind because it was the same thought that was going through his. He didn't want to say good-bye.

"Logan, I want to thank you for your hospitality. You've been the most gracious host."

Walking over to him and letting the grass slip from her fingers, she put both arms around him and hugged him as tightly as she could. "You're welcome. I just want you to know that you've been a real blessing in my time of need. Do you have to move on so soon?" "I do, Logan. It's best that I do for right now. It's not anything you did last night. I was as much to blame for that as you; please believe me."

"If it's not anything I did, then what?"

"It's best that you don't know. I just have to move on for now, but I swear I'll be back." Reaching into his pack, he fumbled around until he selected the right ones. "Here, take these."

"What is it, Daniel? They're rocks—shiny ones, but rocks," Logan said.

"Not just any rocks, but precious gemstones. They're worth. . . I don't know. . . a lot. They're worth a lot of money and are good for trading for things. You keep it and use it when you need to, okay?" "Better take them back, Daniel, you might need them for yourself."

"I've got plenty in my sack, too many in fact."

"Thank you, Daniel. I'll trade with them the next time we go to town. I'd like to buy some curtains I saw in a store that would really brighten up my kitchen. Thank you."

Daniel took Logan in his arms and leaned down to give her a passionate kiss on the lips that said more than words could have said. She offered no resistance, but gave in to the same passion.

"Is there anything I can do to help you, Daniel, with whoever is chasing you?"

"I didn't say anyone was chasing me."

"You don't need to, I can tell someone is after you. It's okay though. I trust you. I know that whatever it is, it will work out best for you."

"You have helped in ways you wouldn't believe. You've lifted my spirits and given me hope. I promise I'll be back when the time is right."

By this time, Logan was in tears. The drops landed on her dress and soaked into the blue and white checkered material. She couldn't hold her emotions back any longer. She was going to miss Daniel, much more than she realized, but she was a strong woman and would endure until he returned. She watched him leave on a trail not far from her cabin that made its way into the mountains. She could see him get smaller and smaller as he eventually reached the tree line. He turned and waved to her, not much more than a speck in the distance, and then he was out of sight.

Logan fell to her knees on the wet ground and cried some more as her body shook from her emotions. She almost felt like running after him, but knew that wouldn't help either of them. He had to do what he was doing and she had to raise and protect her children. She had faith that he would be kept safe and that he would return to her. She would pray for him every day and wait.

Eighteen

The Druid population, which was small, kept to themselves as much as possible. They were completing their duty to protect the MacGows. Activity of the Enlightened Ones had increased recently, and they knew they had to be a little bit more diligent in their efforts. They would mostly keep to themselves doing their farming and odd jobs around the area. They were not interested in getting rich or in excess gain, but would use only the resources they needed day by day, just enough to eat and enough to trade and barter with. They had constructed two large cabins just northwest of Forfar and lived modest lives. They caused no trouble and tried not to draw attention to themselves. Although they were active, it was a quiet and subdued form of subterfuge that they resorted to. They were well able to defend themselves and were very skilled warriors in spite of their looks. The Druid population had had hundreds of years of training and had developed the heart of gentle warriors. They were not boastful braggarts, but looked at killing a foe simply as a necessary act of nature itself. They thought neither bad or good about the act, but treated it as a part of the life cycle. They had the desire to survive and protect themselves and family and to cause hurt to no one. They were also ready to get back to their own normal lifestyle and worship at their groves with their families.

"Sean, we must act to prevent these Enlightened Ones from fulfilling their goals. They are a complete disruption of normal development in this society."

"I know, James. We will do everything within our powers to contain them and push their progress back. We will act without their knowledge of us and lead our lives as if we are attending to our own affairs. We will continue our struggle until the last of us are dead," Sean concluded.

"We pledge our lives and all that we possess to that cause," James said.

The Druids prepared for their monthly ritual in the field near their homes. The bonfire was ready to be lit, and all the Druids assigned to the area were in attendance except the ones guarding the MacGow home. These were rituals that had been performed for hundreds of years. This was something that was not allowed to become neglected, but was held in high regard among those called Druid. They were worshiping the way their forefathers had so many times in the past and they would pass it on to their children and grandchildren. Druids were born leaders in all societies they were involved in. They were simply born to rule, and they were people to be reverenced.

"Since our history is by oral tradition, I will take this opportunity to teach about our people and some of the missions that we have ventured into. We are Celts by every facet of the word. We are proud of our Celtic heritage and have defended it from Julius Caesar to our present circumstances. As most of you know, we have been pushed to the edge of our existence and struggle to survive this day. Our power has diminished, but the remainder of us stand strong to fulfill our goals and purposes.We hold our oak groves as sacred, which is why we meet, even this night, in those same groves. We receive wisdom from the earth through these oak groves. Always hold them sacred in your lives as well," Sean said with emotion in his voice.

"Those of you who have never worshiped in the stone circles would be wise to seek them out and place yourself in their midst. I have worshiped at Stonehenge with my brothers there and also at Castlerigg in Cumbia.I have traveled to the Isle of Lewis and beheld the world through the forty standing stones of Callanish. I received much knowledge there and hold that place to be of special importance to my soul. I urge you to make the journey," Sean expounded.

"My brothers, we have a most important task ahead of us at this present time. We are protecting some who are not really one of us, but are a priority nonetheless. I speak of the MacGows.You have all performed well to this point, but we have unfinished business to attend to that may require your very lives. This is the Druid way. We are on the front lines of life, and that sometimes means giving everything we have to defeat the enemy. None are braver than we are, and none of us will fail. Our enemy is an old foe that we have battled for many generations. I hope you will all stand and be counted as Druids and not shame yourselves or your own families. Peace be unto you," Sean concluded.

As morning filtered through the mist that hung over the valley, Malcolm was out walking through his property, surveying all that was his and thinking back to his father and the life that had been provided for him. The land that Malcolm had inherited was precious to him as well as the memories that had been made through the years. He could see himself running through the fields and chasing his brother Daniel down to the creek where they had often fished together. Their father would bait their hooks for them until they could master it for themselves. This same creek was almost like another family member and he couldn't think of giving it up any more than giving up his own brother. The deer that ran across the far end of the meadow, were part of a daily ritual— sometimes even getting close enough to hand feed.There was even a time when his mother would take them out for a gathering of food and dance; she would spread out a blanket, and they would all sit and enjoy the day. Father would play the fiddle, and they would all sing the old Scottish songs, some even in Gaelic. There were just too many memories in this place, and it had become imbedded in Malcolm's very soul. He would pass it on to Ian, who would in turn pass it to his children. More memories were to be had on this piece of earth.

Malcolm thought about how life would change if Kate found it in her heart to settle down with him— they could be together the rest of their lives. He thought about how wonderful life would be for them both, different at first and maybe even a little scary as they got to know each other more on a day-to-day basis instead of just a dating relationship. Malcolm knew it would be well worth it, and he would do whatever necessary to make it work and to bring joy to the woman he had fallen in love with. If only she would commit to him and help him make it successful. He knew it would take both of them trying, but it would work. With the love he felt for her, he was committed to her happiness. She filled every void in his life like no one else ever had. He knew he sometimes made her uncomfortable by his constant show of affection, but he just could not hold it in. She brought forth from him love that he didn't know he possessed. It was all given to her as an offering of his undying devotion.Malcolm was willing to provide her with children if she so desired and take on any responsibility for her that she required of him.

After his long walk, Malcolm made his way back to the forge to start another day of weapons making and lessons for his clients. He truly enjoyed the camaraderie of the people who frequented his forge and looked at them as friends and people he loved being around. He provided a service that they needed and appreciated. This day was no different. He saw a man leading his horse to the forge, probably because of horseshoe problems. The horse limped a bit, but was fine otherwise. There were others anxiously awaiting the day when their swords or shields would be ready, as a child would wait for a present. Highlanders would come down from the hills to have their weapons made by the master sword maker Malcolm MacGow because they knew of his reputation and his skill at making a great sword. Sometimes, they would even bypass their own blacksmith to have Malcolm make one for them. Business was good, and Ian was going to be a great sword maker himself. This skill had been passed down to Malcolm from his father whom he counted as a better sword maker than himself. His father, Robert, had actually used them in battle and had put them to the test in real life. Fortunately, he had also survived. Malcolm still had that famous sword hung over his fireplace mantle. Ian was now in the forge, making ready for the day's work. He never missed a day of work except once when he had gone hunting and had refused to stop until he had killed a deer that he had chased until nightfall.It had taken him farther than he had planned, and when he finally did make the kill, he had a long day's journey back to haul the carcass. Other than that time, he had been a faithful worker. Malcolm had forgiven him for that one time though. He knew he'd get to taste the best venison anyone could eat, prepared by his son, the part-time chef.

"Mr. MacGow, good morning. I'd like to talk to you, if you have the time."

Malcolm looked at the fellow but did not recognize him. "Do I know you, sir?" Malcolm asked.

"No, we've never met, but I know of you. I hear you're a pretty good blacksmith."

"I've been accused of that," Malcolm said.

"I represent a group of investors in London, and they're interested in your property. We could . . ."

Malcolm interrupted him. "I'm not interested in selling, sir. Have a good day."

"But you haven't heard my offer. I can assure you it's substantial.""Still not selling. I've got a lot of work to do, so good day to you," Malcolm said, annoyed.

"Mr. MacGow, it's worth 5,000 pounds to us, more money than you've ever seen. What do you say now?"

"Still not for sale. I'm going to insist that you leave now, sir," Malcolm said in a stern voice.

"You'll regret this MacGow, mark my word . . . You'll rue this day."

Malcolm didn't take too kindly to the threat delivered to him by this spindly little man, but saw no way he could physically be hurt by him. The man walked hurriedly away back toward where his carriage was parked, looking back several times with a comically contorted face. Malcolm would have thought it funny except for the outrageous offer presented to him. He thought about the amount of money in question and all that it could buy. The man was right; it was more money than he had ever seen in his lifetime, but he thought it too good to be true. His land was worth more than money could buy. His father had nurtured this land and Malcolm was going to make sure that Ian had his part of it as well. Money would be spent eventually and it would all be gone, but land—it had lasting power for future generations. Malcolm was not displeased with his decision.

Malcolm relayed the occurrence to Ian, who thought of his dad as a man with principle who would do the right thing and was proud of him. Ian couldn't imagine going anywhere else or doing any other work. This was his home too, and he wanted to stay.He thought about his uncle, Daniel, who had traveled to the colonies to start a new life, but for him, it was Forfar.

After a hard day's work, Malcolm and Ian called it a day and prepared for supper, which Ian would cook. Malcolm always enjoyed the end of the day because he knew Ian would always come up with a dish or two that would surprise him. Tonight proved to be no exception. Malcolm had eaten to his heart's content, and he knew he would pay for it later, but for now he was in heaven.

Malcolm decided to enjoy a pipe before turning in and strolled out onto the porch to savor the night air. It was dark, but the clouds could still be seen from the moonlight as they passed overhead. Someone getting home late galloped down the road as an owl hooted in the distance.

"Is that English tobacco or homegrown?" came a voice from behind the pine tree to the side of the house.

Malcolm jumped and nearly dropped his pipe at the sound of the voice. "Who's there?" Malcolm demanded.

"Sorry to disturb you, Malcolm. It is I, Sean. Please forgive my intrusion this night."

"Can't you just knock on the door like a normal visitor?"

"I desire to stay out of the sight of others who might be watching for, shall we say, reasons not in your best interests. The fellow who you talked to this afternoon—do you know him?"

"No, never seen him before. He wanted to buy my land. I told him no."

"After he left you, he paid a visit to Mr. Kevin Howard. Mr. Howard was quite upset with the fellow. Malcolm, they want you off this land, you know. They're getting desperate and will even pay to have you out. How much did they offer?"

"5,000 pounds."

"That's a lot of money. You did well, Malcolm. They will begin to play rougher now. You must be ready for that. Something has them concerned. They are trying to beat the clock. They are on a time schedule of some kind," Sean said. "We now have a list of the agitators in this area who belong to the Enlightened Ones organization. The book we took from the MacGregor house was invaluable. They keep good records."

"They must be crazy to think they can recruit the world and make everyone little crazies like themselves," Malcolm said.

"Well, they sometimes get people in a bind or delicate situation where the people have no choice but to join or risk exposure for maybe an illegal business deal or some other embarrassing situation that they just can't let others know about. They are forced to serve or lose their reputation or even go to jail. They join up and sell their souls to keep their positions in society," Sean said.

"I'm not selling my land for any reason, and I'm going to bed now. I have a busy day ahead of me tomorrow. Good night, Sean.""Good night, Malcolm. Stay alert."

Malcolm finished his pipe and knocked the ashes from the bowl as he thought about Sean's words. Heading back into the house, he noticed that Ian had already fallen asleep and was snoring like a wood saw. He joined him and fell asleep with the thoughts of all the day's activities but more importantly, getting together with Kate tomorrow.

After breakfast, Malcolm was eager to get on the road to see Kate, who was meeting him at a place called Tiger Well Road. Malcolm arrived first for he had learned his lesson awhile back—not to be late for Kate. She arrived soon after. After greeting each other in their customary fashion, they were on their way to an eating place that neither had visited before. It was quite a few miles from where they lived, but they didn't mind the trip as they were with each other and enjoying one another immensely.Upon arriving at their destination, they entered the establishment and found a table in the corner. Drinks were ordered and they looked into each other's eyes and just smiled since each knew what the other was thinking. They could read each other like a book as their love emanated from their faces and shown like a bright light upon one other.

Words were not necessary. They communicated their thoughts as if spoken in a loud voice. Kate became playful and slipped her foot up to the lap of Malcolm and they sat there as if everything was normal. Malcolm could hardly keep from exploding and grabbing Kate for a kissing session that would have made a spectacle out of them both. He held back though, and tried to control his breathing and put on a calm and relaxed pose to the others who were in the tavern with them. He was glad that the food had arrived. She would now have to concentrate on eating and give him time to come down from the place she had sent him emotionally.

They finished their lunch and headed toward the door. Holding hands, they walked to the carriage, enjoying each other and the great day that they were experiencing. The ride back was pleasant as they sat close to one another and enjoyed the touch of each other. Kate once more attacked Malcolm's ear with her signature ear kiss that drove Malcolm crazy, but which he loved receiving from Kate. Arriving back at Kate's carriage, they kissed with more passion than Malcolm could ever remember as they drove each other to ecstasy. How could it get any better, Malcolm thought.

"Malcolm, I adore you more than ever," Kate exclaimed.

The look on her face and in her eyes told the whole story. That looksaid it all for Malcolm.

"I love you, Kate. I love you more every time I get to see you anew. You will always be the only girl for me. My desire is for you alone. You are so wonderful," Malcolm said.

"I love you too, Malcolm."

As they headed back toward Forfar, Malcolm was ahead of Kate by several hundred yards. He came upon another carriage that was moving considerably slower, and he slowed as well. As he was exercising patience, he heard a noise coming from behind him like thundering hoofs running from a ghost. It was Kate! She was whipping her horse and getting every bit of speed she could get from her carriage. Malcolm was dumbfounded and wondered why she was going so fast. Maybe she was late for an appointment or just wanted to see what her horse could do. Either way, it was not a safe thing to do on this kind of road. She was gone in a few seconds as she passed Malcolm and the other carriage and left them in a cloud of dust. Malcolm was angry as well as upset because of her safety. It was a reckless thing to do.

Malcolm made it home and was still upset over Kate's behavior. It didn't change his love for her, but revealed another side of her that was unknown to him. Malcolm unhitched his horse and put his apron on as he made his way to the forge to give Ian a hand with the orders. Ian was doing well, turning out the swords and odd jobs in record time. It was good to be able to have a capable assistant and son to take the pressure off. Ian had a great future ahead of him in this business.

Malcolm finished off the rest of the day by giving lessons and putting the finishing touches on a special sword for one of the local clan members. Malcolm was the only one who could be trusted to do special work because of the skills he had gained over the many years. Ian would one day take up that mantle as well. As darkness approached, they decided to call it a day and head for the house. Several customers had paid for their services, and Malcolm was glad for the extra money today. He still had Kate on his mind though and worried about her and her out-of-character tirade earlier that day. He figured she would tell him later why she had acted the way she did.

The next day, Ian and Malcolm talked about the day's activities and planned their day accordingly. Ian mentioned that he would like to try his hand at the Highland games in Breamar the next time they were held. "Do you think you're ready to compete at that level, son?" Malcolm asked.

"I'd like to find out. I've been practicing in my spare time and building up my strength for the events," Ian said.

"Strength is important, but so is timing. If you don't release the object on time, it won't matter how strong you are. You do understand that, don't you?"

"Yes, I do. I actually set up targets to throw to as a way of getting my timing just right. I've only had a few go astray."

"Well, I'll tell you what: the next game they have there, we'll both go and I'll cheer you on. How's that sound? I hope it won't make you nervous."

"It's a deal. Hey, why don't you enter as well?" Ian asked. "So if both of us get laid up, who'll run the forge? No, one MacGow is enough. You do it."

"Makes sense. Thanks for backing me, Dad," Ian thankfully said.

Kate had arrived for her usual lesson and looked a little like she had just dropped a pale eggs and broken them all. She had a different countenance on her face.

"Good morning, Kate. Everything alright?"

"I guess. I have something for you to read first." Kate handed Malcolm a folded up note and asked him to read it. He unfolded the letter and sat down on a log nearby, as did Kate.

> *It's 6:45 p.m. and ever since I saw you this afternoon, I am feeling a cross between sadness and happiness. How can that be, you wonder? It was because of my erraticdriving this afternoon. I know*

you will respond concerning my irresponsible act.Unfortunately, my actions made me realize, based upon how you look out for me, that you really do care for me that much. Why can't I comprehend that you can have such deep feelings for me? I realize you do to a certain degree, but I guess I just figured eventually they would dwindle. I have such a difficult time trusting that such feelings could be sincere. I know I fill a void in your heart and soul. I guess I just can't believe you want to keep risking your reputation and clientele to be with me. Meeting you and pursuing this relationship has been the best thing to happen to me. I feel there is a greater forcethan me that keeps me drawn to you. I am letting my heart direct me, which I have never had the ability to do before. When I am with you, I feel so at ease, so warm, so attracted,which translates to happiness. I never want the time we spend together to end. I wonder if I could ever tire of you. Although you are adventuresome, I still feel that your conservativeness, or cautiousness, keeps us grounded. I tend to get too playful, and I get too engrossed in the moment, which can be dangerous. You keep my spirit alive. You have given me the ability to experience a part of love that men and women share.I care about you and that love I feel growing on a daily basis. It's such a wonderful thing. I never knew it could feel this great. You have come to show me another side of life. I never knew fantasies could be dreamed of. I never knew they could become a reality.

You are real and you are my fantasy. I love you!

After Malcolm finished reading the letter, he looked at Kate and told her he loved her. He was so elated that she would put into writing how she felt about him and them. He absolutely loved what she had done— she had expressed herself and her love for him. He knew he had a special girl and wanted her even more now.

"Marry me, Kate! I love you so much."

"I just can't marry you; we have other commitments in our personal lives to attend to," she said.

"You mean everything in the world to me, Kate. You know that." "Let's wait and see. I do want to be with you, but I don't want to marry. Try and understand," Kate said.

Malcolm did understand, only too well. He hoped for some way to get around the problems so they could be united. He wished no one any harm or for danger to play a part in their coming together, but he wanted the circumstances to change. Malcolm was willing to give up everything for Kate. He had never met anyone like her, not ever. She was the one.

Over the next few days, Malcolm was busy with the forge, and Kate had her responsibilities to attend to. The weekend came and went, and by Tuesday, Malcolm was anxious to meet Kate again. He hadn't seen her for four days and missed her badly. They met at Beltane's once more, but this time Malcolm was on time, unlike the first meeting there when Kate had gotten extremely upset because he was late. Kate came over to Malcolm's carriage and got in. She did not want to touch or kiss him. "I have something to say, and it's not easy. I want to break up with you. I don't feel about you the way I said I did," Kate said, not looking directly at Malcolm.

"I don't understand, Kate. Why? I thought you loved me." "I was just upset with my fiancé, that's all. I don't want to hurt you, Malcolm, but we can't keep doing what we've been doing."

Malcolm slowly touched her hand, and eventually she responded by holding his fingers and then his hand. Malcolm became very emotional and started to cry. He sniffed a few times and talked through sobbing words as he tried to make sense of this situation. "How can you do this? I love you, Kate. You know that."

"The pressure of keeping this whole thing a secret is taking its toll on me. I need to get out from under the sneaking around and looking over my shoulder all the time. We can still be friends, but I must stop the relationship as we know it. Please try and understand, Malcolm," Kate said.

Malcolm told her how much she meant to him and that they could work it out somehow. As he talked to her, he slowly kept touching her hands and then her arm. Moving closer to her, he held her a little bit more, and before they knew it, their lips met again and they kissed each other. The magic of their kisses caused them both to melt into each other's arms as their breath exchanges sealed the wonderful sensation that only their lips could accomplish. They both knew that their lips were made only for each other. No other person had ever done for them what they did to each other. Malcolm could not keep his eyes from filling, tears dropping to his chin and onto his clothing. He was more emotional than most men, but that's just the way he was. He wasn't ashamed of his sensitivity. He wasn't ashamed to show this side of himself to Kate. He wasn't hiding anything from her. He wanted her to know exactly who he was. He bared it all for her.

Malcolm promised to back off from the relationship, and they agreed to see each other, but on a different level. Malcolm didn't want her to feel any pressure of meeting him or having to continue to do things that made her nervous. She would continue to come by the stables and train her horse with Malcolm. She didn't need to give that up. Malcolm loved seeing her every chance he could. The time they spent together was still a time for Malcolm to confess his love to her and make promises to her for the future. He was not about to give up. He was committed to the end because she was worth every sacrifice he would make for themselves. He would hold out hope . . . forever.

As the days in the month moved on, they continued their horseback lessons and an occasional "chance" meeting in the area. On two separate occasions, after one of her lessons, she got Malcolm alone and gave him a kiss on the lips only for a few fleeting seconds and then left. They were kisses that she initiated that said to Malcolm that she still wanted him but "damn the circumstances." About a week and a half after the last kiss, they met for the last time in a more social and public place. They were together for a few hours and said good-bye, but after this time, they never met again. She stopped her horseback lessons, and there was no contact from that point on. Even though Malcolm tried to see her, he was never able to be with her again. He was hurt beyond belief. She had decided not to make contact with him or see him again. Malcolm, being the sensitive person he was, cried for her every day. He had never missed anyone like he missed Kate. He played their relationship over and over in his mind every day and tried to figure out why it hadn't worked. Losing her was like having his very soul ripped from his being; he was now incomplete as a man and a person. He was not whole, and there was nothing to replace her, not ever.

Malcolm's life was basically over in one way. Yes, he still had his loving son and his business, to attend to, but the love of a woman was different from other family love. She had come into his life at a time that he wasn't expecting to be in a relationship, looking to date anyone or get involved with anyone special. It just happened though. From the moment he saw her, he knew she was different and would be someone whom he could not just walk away from or forget. He was right, more right than anything he had ever thought about before. She had grown on him until he fell totally in love with her, flaws and all. He often told her how hard it was to even put into words how he felt. There just had not been adequate meaning for how he felt about her. All he could do now was wait . . . wait until she wanted to come back to him. He would never give up on them and would forever be patient and wait for her return. He believed that the circumstances would one day change, and he would take her back even if he had to get down on his hands and knees. She was that rare and precious gem that only comes around once in life, and he would forever be there for her. If only she knew what he was going through, how his very soul was tortured daily from not having her in his life. This was his Hell on earth.

"Dad, the Widow MacPhorich dropped off my new kilt today. Take a look," Ian said. Ian, wearing his new kilt, modeled it for Malcolm. Malcolm thought the widow had done an excellent job; he had known she was capable and she hadn't disappointed.

"She did great work on that kilt, Ian. I didn't even know you had ordered it though. You sure did surprise me on this."

"I took your advice and went ahead and had it done. I did need a new one, and just look at it! It's beautiful, " Ian said.

"Did you pay her well, son?

"Aye. Used some of my savings and paid her for the trip over here also," Ian said.

"Good. She's been a friend of the family for as long as I can remember. She made my kilt as well."

As Malcolm and Ian conversed, a loud knock on the door sounded. Malcolm got up from his chair and walked toward the door, wondering who could be needing his attention that badly.

"Good day, sir. I am hereby serving notice on you that your house and property has been forfeited to the local government of this region and is to be vacated in ten days time."

"Wait a minute. What are you talking about? Why is my property being taken?" Malcolm wanted to know. "You've no right to my land; I've broken no laws."

"I am only the messenger. It's all spelled out in the papers. Good day, sir."

The messenger quickly retreated from the property and mounted his horse. As Malcolm shut the door, he started reading over the papers."It says here that I have been found aiding a known enemy of the region that has ties to those usurping authority over the local government and that our property is forfeited for public auction. They're accusing the dead Druid of crimes against the government, and they say that I'm connected to that same group."

"What are we going to do, Dad?" Ian asked. "We're not giving up our land and all we've worked for, are we?"

"No, we're not. I'm going down to talk to that magistrate right now. Saddle my horse," Malcolm told Ian.

As Malcolm arrived at the Tolbooth, he hitched his horse to a post and walked up to the gate. Coming out from the building was a man that Malcolm had never seen before. He was dressed in a fancy official uniform.

"We've been expecting you, Mr. MacGow. I'm William Blake, the new magistrate."

"But what happened to Mr. Falconer? He's been here for years." "Mr. Falconer was getting soft, too comfortable. He was a bit too friendly with you locals. It's now time we apply the law to the lawless." "I'm not the lawless, Mr. Blake, and you know it."

"Please come inside. I've someone here who would like to see you," the magistrate said.

As Malcolm made his way inside, the magistrate and another guard escorted him down through a maze of corridors to a holding cell room. At the far end was another guard in front of a cell. As Malcolm approached, he slowly looked inside and saw a man in the shadows. The guard held the lantern up so that the light would shine into the cell."Louis . . . what have you done to him?" Malcolm demanded. "Mr. Mar, or should we just call him the Druid, resisted arrest and had to be subdued. He's resting better now, I believe," Mr. Blake said. "You should count yourself as lucky that you only have to give up your property and not your life like this Druid. Okay, we better go. The Druid needs his rest," Mr. Blake said.

As they marched away from the cell back up the corridor, Louis Mar yelled as loud as he could with his weakened voice, "They're coming, Malcolm . . . they're coming."

"The only one coming for him is the executioner," Mr. Blake said. "Release him to me so I can take care of his wounds. I promise to have him back for his trial," Malcolm said.

"That's not possible. I'll not have two lawbreakers running loose in my town. You have ten days to vacate.You better start packing," Mr. Blake said.

Nineteen

Adam made it back to the Salem establishment, but kept a low profile for the time being. He knew he was alone now since his Druid brothers had been killed in service. He still was going to find a way to help Daniel who was somewhere in the wilderness heading south. After several days of mingling with some of the locals, he learned that several more people had been put to death for witchcraft. Mr. Higginbottom was staying busy with this charade of his. The Enlightened Ones were carrying out their diabolical scheme and fooling people as they went. Adam thought about what a hypocritical township Salem was. The Indians called it Naumkeag, Comfort Haven. The name, Salem, was short for Jerusalem, Hebrew for peace. What peace did the victims of this cruel plot have, being tortured to death for committing no crime whatsoever?

This powerful criminal group had to be stopped and normalcy restored to this region. Justice had to prevail eventually for the sake of the innocents. Adam knew that there were good people here who disagreed with what was going on, but they had no voice in the proceedings, and some were scared for their own safety. Adam would keep his eyes and ears open and hope that he could find a way to make it safe for Daniel's return. Adam would spend a lot of time in the tavern and businesses around town. He would talk to only those people he felt were trustworthy so as not to get himself in trouble. He was in a position that he had never been in before, by himself in a foreign country.

The weeks spent hunting and living off of the land had calmed Daniel considerably. No one had seen him. He had made contact with only a few

Indians doing the same thing he was— making a living. He had explored much of the area all the way over the big mountains and down to the great river, Hudson. This was truly beautiful country. Daniel was amazed at this great land.There was so much big game and a quiet solitude that reminded him of the remote parts of his native Scotland. He lacked for nothing.Nothing, that is, but Logan. She was on his mind a lot. He wanted to go back to see her, but wasn't sure of the timing. Daniel often thought about traveling west as far as he could go, just to see what was on the other end of this great land. Most of the Indian tribes he had encountered had been friendly enough. They would chide him about his Scottish accent, which was so different from the English they were used to. Daniel didn't mind the teasing and would find something about them to poke fun at.He had the ability to get along with them because of his respect for them. They sensed Daniel's respect.

The solitude Daniel found appealing, but it was time he thought about heading back east to see Logan. He had been out here for several months, and he missed his friends back in Salem.He knew he couldn't go back there right now, but he wanted to get in touch with Adam.Winter was ready to move in, and he wanted to be home before that happened. Winter could be very harsh in this part of the country, and he wanted to be in his cabin with his fireplace and enough meat to last him through the winter. He had stored plenty from his hunts this past autumn, but he was sure the authorities would have confiscated it all by now. That made Daniel mad. He had hunted for all those weeks and lost it to that crook Higginbottom.The more he thought about it, the more he wanted to get back to Logan and familiar places. He also felt obligated to Adam the Druid, who was supposed to watch over him, and now was alone as well. He owed Adam a lot for saving his life and for just being there for him through the tough times. Daniel realized he wasn't as alone as he thought when he put it in this perspective.

As the next morning came with a colder than usual foggy day, Daniel knew it was time. It was time to head back. He packed his gear and the few hides he had managed to gather from his kills and said good-bye to this place he had called home for the past months. He wanted a roof over his head and a fireplace to cook in when the snows blanketed the ground. A few weeks back, Daniel had traded with one of the Indian braves for a horse, which would come in handy in transporting his furs and other supplies back east. He thought it good that he was able to walk into the wilderness on foot and come out on horseback. He knew he had managed well. The trip back would be faster and less tiresome on the horse. He figured he could make it to Logan's cabin in four days. He was extremely anxious to see her and wanted to know if the time away had made any impact on her. For him it had. He missed her very much and thought about her every day. It scared him that he couldn't just forget her and move on, but she had gotten under his emotional skin, and that was a new feeling for Daniel. He would find out in a few days what it all meant. As the days moved on, Daniel came nearer to civilization. The Indian roads became wider and wagon wheel ruts appeared. This was not the way he had come, but this road was easier to travel. He knew he could find Logan's place with no problem. Then one day he came upon a group of folks in wagons and on horseback, some walking and carrying sacks over their shoulders.

"Good day. Where you headed?" Daniel asked.

"Out that way." The man on horseback pointed west.

"There's good land that way; just respect it and the people you come upon," Daniel said.

"I guess Old Betsy here will see who gets respected." The man pawed his musket and spit tobacco on the ground in front of him. "You're going to need all the luck you can get with that attitude," Daniel said to himself as he rode on past the settlers. Looking back on them some distance away now, he felt sorry for the ones traveling with such an ignorant and overbearing leader. It wasn't going to be an easy time for them in this harsh environment. They would just have to learn the hard way if they survived.

Coming down off of the mountain, Daniel found a path that he knew would lead to Logan's cabin. He had to duck under branches as he traveled a footpath through the dense foliage. In the distance, he could see smoke that he knew was coming from Logan's fireplace. I wonder if she's cooking that rabbit stew she does so well, he thought. As he neared the cabin clearing, he saw the chimney and then the entire cabin. He could see the children nearby playing a game as they ran after each other, yelling something that he couldn't make out. He trotted closer and was just ready to give a whooping call to announce himself when . . . BANG! Daniel felt a burning sensation as he fell from his horse. Blood was flowing from a wound in his left shoulder, and he felt like a sledgehammer had hit him. He lay on the ground looking up at the graying sky, the wind blowing across his face and swirls of dust kicking up around him. He raised his head just enough to see a man clad in buckskin pants and, deerskin jacket walking up to him with, toting a musket with smoke still seeping from the barrel. "Jack Bryson," Daniel said to himself. "How did he find me?"

"You're so predictable, MacGow. I don't see how you've lasted all this time on your own in the wilderness," Jack said to Daniel. "How did you know I'd be coming back here, you bastard?" "Seems you ran into some very angry men awhile back on this very site. I just waited you out, Daniel, old boy. I'm taking you back this time, but not to worry: the trip for you won't be so unpleasant—you're going back dead over your horse," Jack Bryson said laughing as he began to reload his musket.

"You're just going to kill me like that and think nothing of it?""It'll be easier on all of us, you see. That way I won't have to feed you or worry about you escaping. You've cost me way too much time as it is.Mr. Higginbottom probably thinks I'm dead myself."

As Jack cocked his weapon and aimed it at Daniel, Daniel swore a last oath at Jack Bryson. "May you rot in Hell, you cowardly bastard."A shot rang out, and Jack slowly fell toward the ground next to Daniel. Rolling over on his side the best he could, Daniel looked toward the cabin and saw Logan with her gun still pointed in his direction. She had made a clean shot right at the proper moment and saved Daniel from a certain death. Falling back to the ground, Daniel was unable to move on his own. Logan and the children ran to him and helped him to his feet and slowly walked him to the cabin.

"You're going to be alright, Daniel, and by the way, welcome home," Logan said. The bullet had gone clean through his arm and had not damaged any vital parts. It was going to be awhile until Daniel would be able to move about and get back to a normal behavior.Logan was more than happy to care for him and to have him back.

Logan had started to cry just after she treated Daniel's arm because she realized how close she had come to losing him for good, right in her front yard. In time though, Daniel regained his strength and the use of his arm and began helping Logan around the property. She had missed a man's touch around the place, and he was able to do some of the work that had been neglected for so long. The days turned into weeks, and Daniel was finding that he enjoyed the company of Logan. He also found the answer to his question: how do I feel about Logan?He did not want to leave her again. He wanted her for his wife. In his mind, it was time to settle down and he wanted a woman, this woman, to be with him for the rest of his life.

Several years passed. Daniel and Logan married and conceived two more children, both boys. They named them David and Jamie. Although things were going well where they lived near the Connecticut mountains, Daniel convinced Logan to move back up to the Salem area. Logan was all for it because she craved the fellowship of other women with whom she could converse and share womanly pastimes. Daniel wanted to resume acquaintances with old friends and see if Adam was still in the area. It was settled then: they would move. Daniel thought that after five years, Salem would have forgotten about him and he could blend back into society. He had grown a full beard and his hair was now to his shoulders, helping disguise him to those who might remember him. Everything was packed, and they set out. The trip north was uneventful and a rather pleasant journey for them all. The boys were old enough at three and four to at least realize that they were leaving one place and heading toward another. Logan's other children were able to appreciate the scenery as the days went by. They too looked forward to meeting other children their age.

Nearing Boston, the flow of people became intense with wagons, carriages, and people on horseback, a shock to Logan and the children who were used to almost complete silence except for the wildlife sounds they heard on a daily basis. They looked in awe at this spectacle of humanity before them and wondered if they could adapt.

"Daniel, what's that building over there?' Logan asked.

"That's Harvard.They call it a college. First of its kind here in the colonies," Daniel said. "Logan, don't be taken aback by this big city we're just passing through. It's only a few more miles to Salem where I'm from. It won't seem so big to you later."

"It's all too much, Daniel, but as long as I'm with you, it's okay." They stopped for a food break at a nearby tavern and stuffed themselves for they had missed home cooking since being on the trail for many days. Daniel even had the chance to see a speculator and trade some of his gem rocks for food and other necessities they would need. It was nearly dark when they pulled into Salem.Daniel decided to make camp near the river and wait until the morning to finalize any plans he had. He desperately wanted to see Adam, for he would have the important information that he needed after being away for so long. Daniel did have some trepidation about being back since he was wanted by the law, but he had to see this through. Logan noticed right away how much smaller and quieter Salem was than Boston. She knew she could get used to this place in time.

The next morning brought promise with warm sunshine and a bright sky overhead. The springtime scents of fresh flowers in the countryside permeated the air and gave Daniel a new sense of purpose. The fish were biting as Daniel threw his line into the water for the second time after catching breakfast for at least Logan and the children; one more and they all would eat. A little jelly and some bread and they would have a hearty meal. Logan and the children were up and looking like they were home. Daniel could picture them all together in the cabin as a family enjoying life as God had planned and helping their neighbors as they went. This was supposed to be one of the reasons people came to the colonies: freedom to worship without interference from anyone. He hoped it would become a reality.

After breakfast, Daniel and his family rolled into the heart of Salem. Everything looked pretty much the same except everything looked smaller. It may have been because he was used to the wider spaces of the frontier, so open and vast. Daniel decided to drive to his own home to see what had become of it and what he might do to get it back if necessary. Coming down the road, he could see smoke coming from the chimney and knew that someone was living in it. He was mad at that but his curiosity overrode his anger, at least for the moment. Daniel pulled the wagon in front of the cottage and dismounted, asking Logan to stay there until he knew what the situation was. After knocking on the door several times, he walked around to the side and checked the shed. Inside was a stockpile of furs that were more than he had seen in one hunting season. As Daniel turned to go back to the front of the cabin, he heard the snapping of twigs beneath feet.

"You can hold it right there or face your maker sooner than you thought," came a voice from behind him.

"I'm not trying to steal anything. I'm looking for the owner," Daniel said.

"Well, the owner isn't here, but I'm the caretaker. Who are you?" "I'm Daniel . . . MacMeans," Daniel said with his best lying tongue. Daniel thought there might be a reward for Daniel MacGow, so he played it safe.

"Turn around slowly so I can get a look at you," the man said. Daniel did as he was told and cautiously turned to face the man giving the orders. As his face looked upon the man, he smiled and started chuckling silently, then a little louder until he had a full belly laugh going. "Don't tell me you've become domestic, Adam," Daniel said. ". . . Daniel? Daniel . . . is that you?"

"Aye, it is old friend. Back from the dead as they say." They hugged with all their strength for a long time, releasing pent up emotion.

"I'm sorry, but I didn't recognize you with long hair. You're looking good nonetheless. I'm glad you're back. I almost gave up hope, Daniel." "I have a family, Adam. Come see."

Introductions were made and they all settled into the cottage. After getting caught up on the latest news after the last few years, Daniel was relieved to know that Mr. Higginbottom was out of power again and that the witch trials were over, for the most part. The remaining accused had been set free, and all sentences were acquitted, including Daniel's own. Adam had purchased the cottage with the stones from his bag and had occupied it for Daniel. He had hunted and accumulated the furs for future sale or trade for Daniel also.

The village had become normal once more with only occasional accusations of witchcraft. Mr. Higginbottom had moved to Boston to take a position there in the prosecutor's office. He was not looked upon as an asset to Salem anymore and had made quite a few enemies. It would be years before the people could ever trust each other again and live as neighbors once more. Time was a great healer though, and with the madness over, they could start to rebuild friendships and Christian care. There was plenty of guilt to go around as the local people had acted foolishly and in an unchristian manner. There would be a lot of repentance and re-evaluation of self before the people could look each other in the eye again.

"Daniel, the house is yours and your family's once more. I am not as suited to this type of living as you are. I can only hope that I haven't done too much damage to your lifestyle," Adam said.

"I didn't have much of a style then, I'm afraid. I was just a bachelor living alone and making a living. I think my style will change though with my lovely Logan here to redecorate," Daniel said. "There's one more thing, Adam. I'm releasing you from your obligation to me so you can rejoin your father in Scotland. You have performed in a most gallant and heroic manner, and I couldn't have asked for a better protector. Please accept my thanks and return home to die on your Scottish soil. I don't know if I will ever return, but you must do this."

"I will do it, Daniel. I thank you also for allowing me the honor of serving you. You are more than a mission to me . . . you're my brother. I will miss you sorely."

As life slowly returned to normal for Daniel and his family, he thought about how life had dealt him a hard blow, but also how God had turned it into a blessing with his new family whom he loved so very much. He could have become bitter with having to flee his home and journey into the wilderness to hide, but it had all worked out for him. He was able to continue to build his business of hunting and trapping and even used his gem cache to finance other ventures, which made him rich and a pillar of the community. His children grew, eventually married and had their own families. The MacGow name continued into the future as the family added more and more members. Daniel had made a proud name for himself, coming from Scotland and applying himself and allowing good Scottish Highland blood to flourish and become part of the building of the greatest nation on earth. Adam had taken Daniel's advice and returned to Scotland to be with his father once more. Logan was blessed with many years with Daniel and was never sorry she had made the move to Salem.

TWENTY

"I've no intention of giving up my land without a fight," Malcolm said to Ian. "If I have to stand in my own front yard and weld my sword, I'll hack every man to pieces who sets foot on my property. They'll see what a MacGow sword can really do."

Malcolm was as mad as he had ever been in his life. Corrupt politics had reared its ugly head, usurping the lawful property of one of its citizens. Authorities who answered to no man but the Crown had been installed and were running roughshod over the community. It was an abomination before God and the people. Malcolm was now in the center of the storm because he was fighting against forces that were in direct opposition to the god that he served. It was God that he called upon to help him in this fight. He sought wisdom and direction and a miracle to win the day. He felt as if a heavy weight was upon him. If his god let him down, he would fall. But Malcolm had faith. He would not waver and give a place for the Devil but would trust in God.

"He must be gone in ten days. Our date must be kept if our master is to be revealed to us. It is our sacred day that will be celebrated as our triangle is complete. We will not fail." William Blake was now in charge of the Forfar region of the Enlightened Ones and had Kevin Howard and Alexander Taggart as his lieutenants. They were about to realize what they had strived for these many years. They had recruited some twenty-five additional constables to enforce the confiscation of Malcolm's property. They were taking no chances and wanted to overwhelm him if it came to that. They meant to have that land.

As the days wore on, they were just one day short of the ten-day deadline, and Malcolm had not responded. He had worked each day as any other and put it all in God's hands. He had warned Ian about the deadline, but compelled him to go about his business as usual. Even amidst this terrible predicament, Malcolm thought about Kate. She was strongly on his mind and heart. He knew he couldn't ever have a normal life again, not without her. She either completed him or tore him apart. Right now he was incomplete. He had tried to convince her that leaving her fiancé wasn't the worst thing to happen to her. Yes, it would be rough in the beginning as everything was worked out, but it would eventually smooth out. Life would get back to normal, and they could have a happy life filled with love. Malcolm was committed to that end. She wouldn't have it though. She just couldn't take that step. She really was scared and afraid to let go of her current lifestyle and start anew with Malcolm. She would have the most loving partner in her life — someone who would actually show her love on a daily basis. Malcolm didn't have to pretend to love her; it was what he lived for. He would wait forever.

The day ended with no incident. Tomorrow was the deadline. What would Magistrate Blake do? Was he really so serious about this that he would evict Malcolm? Would he not find another way to solve this? Was he bluffing?

Malcolm had his answer early the next morning. As he was making breakfast with Ian, the sound of horses' hooves broke the morning silence. They came to a galloping stop in front of Malcolm's home as Alexander Taggart, one of the chief constables, got off of his horse to present the official paperwork for the eviction. The magistrate was not among the troop, but stayed at the Tolbooth to await the prisoners to be brought in.

"I'd suggest you get back on your horse and make your way back to your hole if you want to see your grandchildren," Malcolm said with a stern voice.

"Your property is now the possession of the local government and you are hereby commanded to remove yourself immediately or risk arrest. Do you understand, Mr. MacGow?"

"Oh, I understand completely, you spineless worm. You may not have my land, and it's you who is trespassing. I'll ask you to leave now, sir."

"Troop, dismount! Prepare to engage subjects," Alexander Taggart commanded. The first line of eight soldiers stood ready to physically take Malcolm by force while the next line of ten stood ready with muskets to repel any weapon attacks. The remaining soldiers stood guard over the horses. Malcolm now unsheathed his Claymore as did Ian, who wielded his basket hilt sword. They knew this could be their end, but they were going out protecting their liberty and freedom from a tyrannical government that they would not bow to. Time seemed to stand still. Malcolm stared at the troops as the troops stared at Malcolm, waiting for their command to advance. Malcolm knew he couldn't take down all the troops, even with Ian at his side. Before all hell broke loose, the ground shook like an underground volcano that was about to explode. As Malcolm looked over the shoulders of Mr. Taggart and his soldiers, men on horseback, many men, more than Malcolm could count, came streaming into the area around the forge. They were kilted Highlanders in full battle garb. They were whooping and hollering and making all sorts of sounds as they rode. They came closer and closer, and before anyone could move, they slashed through the troop of uniformed men. The horses of the troop scattered as the men holding them pulled their own swords in a futile defense. The Highlanders continued to cut down the magistrate's men like cattails in a pond. The carnage was horrific as limbs were cut from bodies and heads rolled.

"Call off your men, Malcolm, and we'll talk this out," Mr. Taggart said.

"They're not my men, Taggart, but they are an answer to my prayer." As the last man in the troop was slain, several of the Highlanders ran and took Mr. Taggart, tying him up like a bale of wool. They placed him on a horse and whisked him away into the surrounding hills. Malcolm remembered what Louis Mar had said when leaving the Tolbooth: "They're coming . . . they're coming." He had meant the Highlanders. Somehow, he had gotten the message out about what the magistrate was going to do.

As Malcolm and Ian put their swords away, they saw another group of Highlanders, led by Sean, coming down the road. They had Louis Mar on horseback with a blanket wrapped around him as he slumped forward, barely able to stay upright. Sean and his group had broken Louis out of the Tolbooth and rescued him.

"Malcolm, you are safe once more. There is no one left to give you trouble. Those in the Tolbooth are leaderless or on the run. We will head to the hills and deal justice to the leaders of this band of hooligans. Live in peace, Malcolm and Ian," Sean said.

The Highlanders carried the bodies of the slain off on the horses they had ridden in on, preparing to dispose of them in the mountains. As Sean and the Highlanders rode by, Malcolm saw William Blake, bound and gagged, being led away with other members of the town who had played a part in scheming to dispossess Malcolm from his land. Malcolm had not expected such an act from God, but he was very thankful for the intervention. Hopefully, things would get back to normal again. His future was secure for the time being, and

Ian could look forward to a future on his own land. As Malcolm looked down to the ground where the battle had just taken place, he noticed a severed hand. On the finger was a ring that was like the ones worn by other members of the Enlightened Ones. It had the familiar lightning bolt design engraved upon it. Malcolm slid it off of the finger and kept it as a reminder of of what they had fought against.

In time, the village did get back to normal. Mr. Falconer had been reassigned to the Tolbooth with a beefed up contingency of his own troops, and he kept the peace. He was a more welcome magistrate for he had grown up in the area and was known by many who lived there. Malcolm's business continued to grow, which kept him busy and happy. Ian met a girl whom he eventually married and had three sons and one daughter. Malcolm lived on with the thought of one day seeing and maybe talking to Kate once more. In spite of the time lapse since their breakup, Malcolm still longed for her just as much as from day one. He knew he would never meet anyone like her again, but then he didn't want to. She had stolen his heart. It was Kate whom he thought about while turning in for the night and when he arose in the morning. He would still cry in secret when no one was around and when he let his thoughts drift to her. Malcolm found it hard, emotionally, to live and breathe without Kate. He prayed for the circumstances to change and invite them back together. He refused to let go. "Kate, come back to me. I miss you so very much. Please keep a place for me in your heart and think about the times we shared together. Think about the kisses we experienced and the touch of our lips as they met on so many occasions, and how we looked into each other's eyes and expressed our fondness for each other. I am always here for you and will wait for you no matter how old we grow to be. When you are too old to do for yourself, I will still confess to you my undying love. I'm never going to let our love die and will do whatever it takes to keep it alive. I will be the guardian of that love and it will be my eternal quest. I will always be willing to lay my life down for you and to do whatever makes you happy. Semper Fidelis. You are my classy lady."

Twenty One

"Taxi! Damn! Can't those drivers see me hailing them?" Rory said, with a slightly angry voice. Rory was soaking wet from the torrential downpour he had been caught in ever since leaving his office twenty minutes ago. It had been one of those days when work kept piling up and computers kept going down with frozen screens. Rory wanted to get home for his childrens' birthdays, which were celebrated together as they were one year and one day apart. Kenna would be ten and Morven would be nine. It was dark outside, and the rain was still coming down in sheets, obscuring the vision of the taxi drivers and making it hard to see the drenched Mr. Rory MacGow. It didn't help any that he was wearing a dark trench coat.

He arrived later than he wanted to, but still in time to enjoy the party for his pride and joy. "Sorry I'm late, honey, had to stay late to finish the big Grigsby deal. If I sell that, it'll provide my biggest commission check this year," Rory said.

"That's okay, I have everything under control. The neighbor kids will be here any minute. Put the candles on the cake," Rory's wife, Heather, said.

Rory and Heather had lived in Salem forever. He came from a long line of MacGows, a line that had been one of the founding families as far as they could tell. They loved Salem and wouldn't think of living anyplace else.

The night went well with the party, and the children received many presents, too many as far as that goes. They were only slightly spoiled—not as bad as some of the other children in the neighborhood, but that was no excuse,

Heather knew. The children were put to bed, and Rory was fast asleep as soon as he hit the pillow. "Good night . . ." Heather knew he hadn't heard her, but she still insisted on wishing him peaceful dreams.

The weekend was here. Saturday morning and no office transactions to contend with today. Rory arose from a restful sleep with renewed energy. Heather was making breakfast for the kids, who were busy watching the Doodle Bops on TV— some adults dressed up in painted costumes who danced and sang simple, corny songs. Rory was going to the library to do some more work on his family tree, adding to information that he had inherited from his father. He had gotten interested in his tree when he attended the Scottish Highland games in North Carolina at Grandfather Mountain. He knew his lineage went back to Scotland or Ireland, but didn't know exactly where. Genealogy was time consuming but interesting work. He knew he would eventually have to travel to get the records he wanted, for some were not on the Internet or in the local library. Rory held his family roots in a very special place in his life. He even thought about buying a kilt to show his dedication to them. He could wear it to other Highland gatherings throughout the year and be prideful of his beginnings.

Rory did very well in his business and met interesting people in the Salem area. He could afford to take off and travel if he needed to and often did. He often took Heather to a beach resort either in California or Florida, and they had been to the Caribbean twice. As much as he loved the beach, he yearned to visit his Celtic roots. Besides, they must have beaches there. He would love to connect his American side with his European side to complete his circle of life. How far he got with this side would determine if and when he would go over there.

The weekend went by fast, and before he knew it, he was on his way to work again. He desperately wanted to close this deal with Mr. Grigsby because he was anticipating a new trip coming up. Heather would be really happy if he took her to one of the Mexican resorts or even South America. If he could time it right, the kids could come along too. Mr.Grigsby wanted to buy the twenty acres overlooking Beverly Harbor for his planned headquarters for universal peace. He was to call it Abraxas. Rory didn't know what that meant, but he did want the commission.After meeting with the board to get approval for the development, it was approved unanimously. Mr. Grigsby would be pleased, and another development would be added to the area skyline. Rory had been promoted to vice-president of his division about a year ago after making the company a ton of money on some of his transactions. He was doing a bang-up job at his position.Rory was making the reservations for his trip in his mind before he got out of the meeting. Everything else from here on out was just details on this transaction.

Rory put in a long day at the office with other smaller jobs he was working on and decided to call it a day. He was getting caught up in the genealogy search for his family and was eager to continue with that. Rory had gotten his car back from the dealer after the call-back on his model and was glad he didn't have to wait on a taxi again. Once at home, he greeted his family and headed off to his computer and his research."Daddy, what's a kilt?" Morven asked. She had heard Rory tell Heather that he might get a kilt because of his heritage, and she was curious.

"Well, it's a colored piece of material that my ancestors wore over in Scotland. It kind of looks like a dress, but it's not. It's what the men wore over there many years ago. Some still wear them at special occasions to show where they came from. Does that answer your question?"

"You're going to wear a dress, Daddy?"

"No, I just told you: it's what the men wore in Scotland. Here, let me show you a picture on the screen here. See those men with the swords? They're wearing kilts. And here, these men are playing bagpipes while they march, and they're wearing kilts. Now do you understand?" As Morven jumped off Rory's lap, she went running from the room to the kitchen, "Mommy, Daddy's going to wear a dress!"

"Okay, I give up. Well, I've got to get back to my studies." Rory continued to research deeper and deeper into the history and lineage of his people until he came upon a man named Daniel MacGow. Rory found out that Daniel had married a girl named Logan and had two children, David and Jamie. "It matches! David had children who connect with my line.That's my David!" Rory said with renewed enthusiasm. "It's like putting a puzzle together and finding a key missing piece."

Rory continued to delve and found that Daniel had a brother in Scotland in the Forfar area on the east coast. "So my people came from Forfar, Scotland. How about that? I wonder why Daniel came to America and Malcolm didn't? This was way back in the 1690's apparently. I wonder what it was like back then?What clan did they belong to?" Rory said to himself. "Well, at least I got it back to Scotland with names and dates. This stuff is fascinating. I have to visit that area. I have to physically be there. I want to walk the very ground that my ancestors trodded. I want to kiss the soil that they were raised on. I've got to tell Heather."

After an exuberant demonstration of excitement, Rory came back down to earth and was able to relate the story to Heather. She was as excited as Rory because she liked it when he was happy; it made her happy.

"Well, do you want to go?" Rory asked Heather.

"Where? To Scotland? Of course, I'd love to go. Could we visit Ireland as well?" Heather asked.

"I guess we could arrange it. Why not?"

Rory made plans for their trip to Scotland, but also continued to research his history. He found a museum that carried records of the area and made more connections to his roots. He was cross-referencing some of the names and noticed that Daniel MacGow was mentioned in connection with the Salem witch trials. He came across a roster of people who had been prosecuted for witchcraft, and on the page right in front of him was Daniel's name. He wondered if it was possible that there were two Daniels, but found that not to be probable. This was a startling development in his search. It just said that Daniel was one of the accused, but no word on what the result of the trial was. Rory knew that Daniel wasn't executed when they had the witch trials because he had his death date recorded, which came after the witch dates. He lived on somehow, married, and had kids. "My ancestor, arrested for witchcraft, I can't believe it. I wonder how he escaped the death penalty. I'm glad he got away. Otherwise, I wouldn't be here," Rory said to himself. In the next few days, Rory met with the board and Mr. Grigsby for the final paper signing. Everyone who had been expected to be at the meeting was there. Pleasantries were exchanged and a lot of handshaking took place. As the seats were filled around the table, papers were passed and checked by lawyers before each, in turn, signed his or her names. As Rory was watching the procession of papers go around the table, he couldn't help but notice the ring on Mr. Grigsby's hand. It was unusual. Rory saw it as a lightning bolt. He wondered what it signified to Mr. Grigsby. After the signing was done and contracts made legal, Rory, for some reason, couldn't help but ask Mr. Grigsby what his ring design meant.

"Oh, thank you for asking, Mr. MacGow. It's a keepsake handed down from my father and from his father. It signifies world peace, which is what my building project is all about, remember," he said to Rory. "Well, it certainly is different, I must admit," Rory said.

They said their goodbyes and went about their business.

Rory stayed busy in his research and was eager to travel to Scotland with Heather and the kids. The day finally arrived for their departure, and they flew from Boston to Edinburgh in anticipation of getting back to Rory's roots.

This was most important to him, for it was not a typical vacation, but a working excursion to seek answers.

Edinburgh was a delight, but Rory was looking forward to the side trip to Forfar. This was like coming home even though he knew no one and no one knew him. He had all of his research papers with dates and names and events that took place so many years ago. Rory had arranged for a rental car for the family, and they started off from Edinburgh to Stirling, Perth, Dundee and finally Forfar. It wasn't that far of a drive, but it surely was beautiful and unlike any place he had been before. The whole trip made his heart beat differently and caused goose bumps to rise on his arms and neck. This was definitely not a simple vacation trip. Anticipation was the word that best described what Rory was experiencing inside, like he was visiting a long lost relative.

As they arrived in town, Rory could see the building referred to as the Tolbooth. He had read all about the history of it and thought back to that time in history and what had taken place there. Rory and his family settled into their accommodations as Rory mapped out his itinerary to explore the area. Heather and the children walked around and looked at the shops while Rory talked to some of the local people and visited the library and museum to see what they could contribute to his findings. Old maps were there, and stories of long ago were recorded for anyone to read. They even had a section for the local witch trials section, much like the one back in Salem. They used the same modus operandi of accusing old defenseless women and subjecting them to various tortures. Forfar had not embraced the history of the witch trials as elaborately as had Salem, which had a museum and monuments dedicated to the poor people who perished for no good reason.

As he talked to various shopkeepers and merchants, he was eventually directed to a farm area a few miles from the city proper but still in Forfar. He rented a bike since it was too far to walk and he needed the exercise anyway. The countryside was beautiful with colorful gardens of many differing flowers, shrubs, and climbing plants. Fragrance seemed to hover in the air as Rory rode along slowly breathing in the scent that was almost spell-binding. For a moment, he thought about living here and what peace that would bring him and his family: no hustle and bustle fighting traffic and crowded streets, no deadlines to meet with nerve jarring pressure and living the way God intended: in a garden setting with nature all around and an open sky above.

As Rory fantasized about this kind of world, he soon came back to reality when the front tire on his bike hit a rut and sent him head over heels into the dirt road. Sprawled out in the road on his back with a broken rim on his bike, he realized that even paradise had pitfalls to contend with. Getting up from the ground and inspecting himself for damage, he felt at least good enough to walk, but the poor bike would have to be carried.

"Nasty fall you took there, lad. Are you alright?" came a voice from the other side of the road.It was a local farmer who was tending his fruit trees and had just climbed down from one of them.

"I believe so. No broken bones, as I can tell," Rory answered. "You must be an American. We can always tell," the man said. "I am an American, but how did you know?"

"Because you all seem to be in a dream world when you get over here, and you lose your sense of direction for a bit, until something like this happens."

"You're good, and you are correct," Rory said.

"I'd be happy to give you a lift back to town; my truck is just on the other side of the orchard here."

"That would be most gracious of you, and I accept."

Rory dragged the bike to the side of the road and hopped the fence to where the man was. Limping just a little, Rory was starting to feel the bruising of his leg and shoulder.

"Looks like you've taken more of a spill than you thought there. Let me take you over to my cottage, and the wife will take a look at your wounds and maybe put some wraps on them."

"Okay, that might be a good idea," Rory said. "By the way, I'm Rory MacGow from Massachusetts. My wife and kids are in town doing some shopping— hopefully not too much," Rory laughed.

"Funny, I'm a MacGow too. I'm Glaschen MacGow. My family has lived here for many generations."

"That's interesting. I'm actually here doing a research on my familywhich I believe was from this area. Would you mind if I ask you some questions on your lineage?" Rory asked.

"Not at all."

Glaschen's wife, Rebecca bandaged Rory's wounds, and they all sat down and went over the charts and papers that Rory carried in his pack. They spread the papers out on the table as Glaschen tried to decipher everything that was before him. Glaschen's wife brought out books from their chests that contained numerous names of family members that went back further than any of them could begin to remember. As the day went on, Rory and Glaschen both concluded that they were indeed related, and Rory had found his missing link to Scotland.

"This is one of the greatest moments of my life!" Rory exclaimed. Rory fell back on the couch in a slumped position with arms dragging and legs spread open as if he had just run a marathon. He felt exhausted as his lungs gasped for air. He was emotionally spent.

Glaschen had collected many writings and books on his family and had preserved everything that had been handed down to him from the previous generations. Rory had the opportunity to read over the history of this family, which was really his family too, and concluded that they truly were the same family.

"Do you realize, Glaschen, that we are the descendants of the same two brothers mentioned in your works here and mine from America? Daniel went to America and Malcolm stayed here. This is so amazing. There's no mention of them ever getting back together in any of our papers. That's somehow sad; don't you think?"

"Aye, it is sad. They must have loved each other, as brothers, but I guess the distance they would have had to travel squelched any reunion they may have thought about. They had their families to provide for and they just couldn't get on a plane and hop over the Atlantic."

"Honey, show him this," Rebecca said to Glaschen. She handed Glaschen a ring from the chest that they kept in a smaller box for jewelry and other small items.

"This ring has been in the family forever also. We don't really know the history of it or if Malcolm or his son wore it or some other family member later on," Glaschen added. As he handed it to Rory, Rory focused on the design of the crest in the ring. He was familiar with it already.

"Glaschen, I just completed a contract back home with a man who had this exact same ring on his hand. This is a lightning bolt, am I right?" Rory asked.

"As far as I can tell, it is. It has to be an old design since this one has been in the family for generations. If you saw it recently in America though, that is rather odd, to say the least."

They could draw no conclusion about the ring at this point. Glaschen suggested that Rory bring the family by tomorrow for a good old family get-together and they would throw a feast that would never be forgotten. That is exactly what they did. Both families united for a good time of reminiscing and reflecting on things that were near to both: how they came to be and where they were headed. Long lost relatives united after more than three-hundred years, related to each other and not knowing it, but coming to that point in time that they both crisscrossed each other's time line and met for the first time.

Malcolm and Daniel had begun a legacy of family that had spannedthe many years of turbulent times in an era when nations were being forged and nations dissolved, both families surviving in their own world and contributing as each person could. Scotland's people were thrown into subjugation in 1746 by their English overlords, while in the colonies, Americans were throwing off the yoke in 1776 to become their own masters.

Malcolm and Daniel had taught their children to obey God and respect their neighbors. They did it in their own countries and made the best of the situations they were in. They both turned out alright. They were both from good Highland stock, even though culturally they were different because of their upbringing. Their DNA was the same though, and they thought of themselves as brothers.

Rory and Glaschen would remain close friends forever and fight the enemies that confronted them on a daily basis. The rules had changed with the modern era they now lived in, but the heart of man was the same. Evil men would always be out there to spread their venom, and the good would be there to meet the challenge of those who would try and take away their freedoms. Glaschen thought about the battles that his long dead descendant, Malcolm, might have fought in his day. Every time he looked at the sword hanging above his fireplace, a sword with the Malcolm MacGow signature on the hilt, he wondered if he too could wield it if he ever needed to.

About the Author

This is my first novel. I had, for many years, contemplated writing a book but didn't think I had enough to say. I am 57 years old, married with two grown children who live in Europe. I was born in Cincinnati, Ohio, but am of southern parents who gave me the traits of their own heritage from which I am very proud. I have lived in Gatlinburg, TN for the past 15 years where I make my home. I am an avid hiker who enjoys the Great Smoky Mountains and just being out in nature.

In writing this novel, I called upon my involvement with the Scottish Highland Games, which I have regularly attended for the past 12 years as part of my heritage. I also am well versed in world and American history. It is my love for Scotland that gave me the encouragement to put pen to paper and see what I had in me as a novelist. I found that the words would flow as if someone were telling me what to write next and where the book should go. My characters came alive to me and I just followed their lead.

CPSIA information can be obtained at www.ICGtesting.com
Printed in the USA
LVOW13s0417280114

371175LV00002B/171/P